Wild California

Other books by Victoria Nelson

The Secret Life of Puppets

My Time in Hawaii

On Writer's Block

*Letters, Drawings and Selected Prose
of Bruno Schulz*
(Co-translator with Walter Arndt)

Wild California

Victoria Nelson

Five Leaves Publications

www.fiveleaves.co.uk

Wild California
by Victoria Nelson

Published in 2004 by Five Leaves Publications,
PO Box 81, Nottingham NG5 4ER
www.fiveleaves.co.uk

Five Leaves acknowledges financial assistance
from Arts Council England

ISBN: 0 907123 84 8

Design and typesetting by Four Sheets Design and Print
Printed in Great Britain

Acknowledgements
These stories originally appeared in *Raritan, Bamboo Ridge* and
Southwest Review. "Bolinas Venus" was first published in a let-
terpress edition by The Greenwood Press under the title *Queen
of Hearts*. Thanks to the Headlands Center for the Arts,
Sausalito, California, for studio space and inspiration while com-
pleting this collection.

The cover illustration, A Glass of Wine, is by Anita Klein,
whose work can be seen on www.anitaklein.com
and at The Boundary Gallery in London.

Contents

Wild California

Months later he was still combing the *Chronicle* front to back (obituaries first), the Marin *Independent Journal* too, but he never found a thing.

The afternoon of the reading, when the Honda Civic's engine failed to turn over, Warren had called for a taxi right away; stray cabs did not routinely cruise the neighbourhoods of his native city, especially not the top of Telegraph Hill. Half an hour later he stepped over a ribbon of cobalt onto a gently rocking Blue & Gold in pleasant anticipation of a soul-cleansing ferry ride across the San Francisco Bay. His duties would be over by nine and he could catch a Golden Gate Transit bus back. He paid for an overpriced Vodka Collins in the ferry's lounge and climbed to the upper deck. Even though the day was sunny, all the old hands, the commuters, stayed down below in the enclosed cabin drinking and reading; only tourists ventured up here. Seating himself on a long wooden bench, Warren took the precaution of zipping up his parka. Once they reached open water, that stiff bay wind would start to bite.

1

Under confused skies the ferry cut through the whitecaps toward the little town on the northern side of the bay. Buoy bells clanged outside the Gate; soon the bay foghorns would join in. From the low western horizon a sharply defined funnel of fog spilled through the Golden Gate, swallowing up the rust-red towers of the bridge; it was heading straight for cloud-shadowed Angel Island and Alcatraz like a long squirt of icing from a decorator's gun. On the Marin side of the bridge, backlit by the muffled sun, a second mile-high fogbank over Wolf Ridge surged down the steep hillside through the section of Sausalito called Hurricane Gulch. In about twenty minutes wave and funnel would meet in the centre of the bay to launch a single blitzkrieg on the East Bay cities of Oakland and Berkeley.

As it always did, this spectacle captured the attention of a group of tourists standing on the deck near Warren. Ranging in age from eight to eighty and dressed in identical beige velour jogging suits, they appeared to be a prosperous Spanish-speaking extended family. Latin American, Warren decided; it was winter down there now. Oblivious to the seagulls that circled low overhead angrily squawking for food and depositing white blotches on their shoulderpads, the family members stood transfixed. Even a blasé native like Warren had to admit the coming of the fog was a thrilling sight, promise of some cosmic adventure forever unfolding just out of reach.

On a more mundane note, he found himself wondering exactly how many people would be showing up for the Sausalito Public Library "Local Heroes" series. That old story about a library reading, how did it go? The writer, discovering his audience is one solitary man in a sea of empty chairs, pumps himself up like a trooper and delivers his best performance — hell, the guy came, didn't he? Halfway through, two police officers walk in, handcuff the man, and lead him away. Unanswered question: Did the writer keep on reading? Would Warren have? Trees falling in the forest, etc.

Acutely aware of his lack of national recognition, Warren was fine with Local Hero — once he had discreetly ascertained that previous and upcoming series readers were either at his level of nonfame or slightly higher — and he felt confident there'd be more than one person in the audience. He'd enjoyed talking on the phone to the brisk young woman, name of Olga, who had booked him. Olga had sounded not at all like a fan; her faintly accented voice carried the implication that there might be something slightly off, gauche even, about Warren. He had found this light note of contempt refreshing and looked forward to meeting her in person. Low-key sentimental fantasy: Olga would be fun, youngish, and maybe up for a drink after the reading. Most everyone he knew in the poetry game lapped up the adoration and concomitant sexual favours of fans, taking it all as no more than their due after an obligatory dorky adolescence and young adulthood. Warren, however, too bad for him, found groupie love nauseating. The gap between what those shining eyes imagined and reality was a Grand Canyon too enormous for his sceptic's psyche to negotiate. The root of all hero worship, an old poet had told him — for once it was something useful — is hostility. Think you're shooting fish in a barrel? Before you know it they've murdered you. As far as Warren was concerned, you ended up murdered anyway, but that was another story. For him the safest bet was always a neutral — in this case, mildly condescending — stranger. Tonight, if it turned out that Olga lived in the City, he'd settle for a ride home.

The ferry closed in on the Sausalito dock and Warren stood up. Before him rose a green hillside dotted with a jumble of wooden Victorians, brown-shingled bungalows, Fifties-era apartment buildings, and faux Mediterranean villas. Nylon parka flapping loudly in the wind like the rotor blades of a helicopter, he crossed the deck to the stairs and disembarked with the throng. On the dock he checked his watch: still plenty of time to make a leisurely stroll down Bridgeway, Sausalito's main drag. The library was located on the other side of town from this tourist combat zone.

He walked past the Italian coffee-house where twenty years before assorted locals — some of them European transplants and some from Marin City, the former World War II shipworkers' ghetto — had whiled away the day dealing coke over the pay phones. Now shiny-helmeted latte-sipping bike racers in spandex and wraparound sunglasses squatted on the sidewalk like giant insects. Thinking of Gregor Samsa and the saucer of milk, Warren knew it was wrong to miss the coke dealers. When they'd been around, especially that dapper character in the Borsolino who bore a striking resemblance to O.J.,

4

he hadn't been able to abide them.

He climbed the hill to the large building that had once been a primary school, walked down its cavernous main hall to the double swinging doors and into the big two-story room that was the library, now filled with neat rows of folding chairs facing an oak lectern. Warren was taking in the breathtaking view of the harbour at the large bay window when a striking blonde in her late twenties with the thinly pencilled eyebrows of an old-time movie star came up. Olga, he assumed, though she did not introduce herself.

Her manner as haughty as it had been over the phone, the woman spoke his name flatly. When Warren nodded, she led him up an open stairway to a little office space behind the stacks on the mezzanine. From behind and below he admired Olga's slender body, decked out in expensive leisure wear. A pair of highly impractical, equally expensive sandals adorned her pedicured feet. Not someone you expected as a public library functionary, even in Marin County (to which the adjective "affluent" was routinely appended). This must be some sort of community service job, he concluded. Olga was the kind of person you would meet, definitely in passing, at a Hamptons cocktail party.

In the office Warren commenced trying to amuse Olga while she rummaged inattentively through a desk drawer. To his dismay, he even heard himself recounting the story of the writer with the single listener and laughing, by himself, at the punchline. Now Olga had found what she was looking for: a pile of brightly coloured buttons in a cardboard box.

Smiling at last — if ironically — she fastened one on his jacket lapel. Warren doubled his chin to read the legend upside down: "Local Hero."

She made a little grimace. "That's the series theme."

"I know." Fingering it, Warren decided to leave the button on. He sat in the office chair as Olga checked the clock impatiently and the room below them slowly filled with people. At five minutes past seven, she motioned him to follow her down the stairs. Olga walked up to the podium, took out a little index card covered with handwriting and read aloud from it with practiced vivacity. She spoke first of the library's upcoming activities, then mentioned Warren by name as "the well-known North Beach poet" and, squinting prettily at her own writing, read off a list of his published books. In a flutter of applause from the mostly middle-aged group, Warren walked to the podium, put down his manuscript pages, and took a sip of the bottled water on the desk.

He had just opened his mouth to begin when the jangle of a cell phone broke the room's expectant stillness. Olga fished a Nokia out of her tiny bag. Instead of shutting it off, she began a hushed conversation that lasted an interminable minute. Ringing off, Olga met Warren's outraged gaze with a moué of apology. She put the phone back in her purse and he lowered his eyes once more. But scarcely had he screwed himself back into declamatory mode than the library's double doors burst dramatically open. A slight, tousled-haired young man in a blue suede windbreaker rushed in. The latecomer slid into the first available seat in the last row — but not before making a respectful little bow to the reader.

Slightly mollified, Warren began the long new unpublished work he was still putting the finishing touches on. Perhaps because the young man's face had taken on exactly the concentrated expression of Warren's own — that of someone attending at the very deepest level — he now found himself actively playing to the newcomer in the back row. It galvanised you, no question, to have this kind of listener. Hairs standing on the back of his neck, Warren found himself sailing through the poem with that rarest of sensations, a small, guarded feeling of wonder at what he almost might have accomplished, given a few more years and brains.

"Thank you," he said finally, turning over the pile of manuscript pages to indicate that the reading was over. The young man in the back pounded his hands together loudly as the rest of the audience politely clapped, then raced up to the podium to pump Warren's hand. "Three years in this country and you are the first poet I have the fortune actually to meet in person. And such a poet. Your style, if a nonnative speaker may be permitted to say so, is exemplary. What did I tell you?" he called back to Olga, who was coming forward with rather a sour smile on her face.

"This is Sergei Slansky," she told Warren. "He has been very anxious to meet you."

Sergei still seemed unnaturally excited. "Of course, I have read many American poets — Stevens, Olson, Bishop, Duncan, Spicer."

"You have excellent taste," Warren said.

Sergei blushed with pleasure. "I once wanted to be critic. Scholar. Anything but what I am — businessman. I would so much like to discuss with you the content of this poem that you read, because it has a great deal of personal interest for me. Tonight, unfortunately, I cannot. Meanwhile please consider me your devoted admirer."

Giving Warren another little bow, he took Olga by the elbow and briskly guided her over to a corner, where he began talking rapidfire in a language Warren assumed was Russian. Every statement Sergei made, however, Olga greeted with escalating disdain; even Warren could make out the angry *nyets* that peppered her responses.

Embarrassed to be listening, he moved out of earshot as a few people pressed forward with copies of his books to sign. Warren sat down at a reading table and obliged, feeling as he always did more an indentured servant of the great American quest for collectibles than an honoured bearer of literary culture. Passing over a battered paperback, a teenage boy asked him, "Did you know Kerouac?" Smiling faintly without looking up, Warren shook his head. People often asked him that kind of question, but the fact was that he was linked with North Beach geographically, not culturally, from the simple accident that the little house on Telegraph Hill his uncle left him years ago overlooked that neighbourhood. Young people had a fierce untutored nostalgia for the old days; they wanted tales of drugs and excess. Beatniks, oh boy! The only literary movement ever to penetrate mass American consciousness, probably solely because of those aspects of it that were spectacularly unliterary. Warren, who had never driven across the continental U.S. high on speed, had been all of twelve the year Jack Kerouac expired. Poetically speaking, he operated in a specialised sub-niche of rarefied aesthetics complicated by ludicrous blood feuds. His own crazy times had consisted mainly of café-ing in the seventies, pretty tame stuff next to the sock-a-delic sixties, strung-out fifties, and fornicating forties of literary San Francisco.

Civilians, he reflected as he signed his name on the book's title page, didn't realise — and why should they? — how radically the texture of writer-and-artist bohemia in America had changed in the late twentieth century. Where Robert Duncan had washed dishes, Warren had gotten a master's degree in creative writing. A life spent in creative writing programs and literary conferences (not that Warren himself, a perennial campus pinch hitter, had even managed to achieve this dubious sinecure with any consistency) offered a great deal more financial stability but was as narrow and colourless as an accountant's, if not more so. Still, the notion of anyone who had spent his twenties and a good part of his thirties simply having fun, as Warren had, seemed exotic enough compared to the packaged pleasures of some of the poetry up-and-comers he knew. Had those sober young individuals in blazers, their fiercest passions focused on wringing every last name-brand letter of recommendation they could out of the system, ever had a moment of absolutely innocent pleasure? The kind of pleasure you could only experience after months and months of doing fuck-all and not caring even the tiniest bit about your career? What was it they'd put together that time at McClure's Beach? The Flying Zazaloffs, a human pyramid of seven or eight drunken people lying on the sand with their legs waving in the air — Kafka again — maybe two at most hoisted overhead (very briefly) on a forest of shaky legs? Much silly laughter. Did you need a nice car, tenure even, if you'd had a Zazaloff youth? Warren didn't have a simple yes or no answer to that question, but he did know that the two experience tracks tended to be mutually exclusionary.

After signing the last book and bidding its owner a civil good night, he looked up to an empty room. The sound of a door being locked came from overhead. Olga appeared on the balcony. There was no sign of Sergei. As she started down the stairs, Warren asked, "Do you by any chance live in the City?"

"No." That was all. Not "Thank you for an inspiring reading," not even "Thank you for coming." Warren discovered that he no longer found Olga's rudeness stimulating; the cell phone incident had cinched that.

"I wonder if you could drop me off downtown at the bus stop? My car's on the fritz and I had to take the ferry over."

She looked at him with weary eyes — female judgment on the kind of feckless fellow who lacked a decent car, or mistaken interpretation of a pass (which it might well have been, had he known her only ten minutes instead of a whole two hours)? "Come on," she said finally. "My car's in the lot."

Feeling like the grocery bagboy, Warren followed her up the back stairs to a hillside parking lot where a late model beige Mercedes Benz sat in solitary splendour. Neither spoke as Olga backed the car expertly out of the lot and guided it down the steep hill to Bridgeway. An odd commotion began in the back seat when she stopped at the intersection. Warren turned around. Throwing off the tartan laprobe that had concealed him, Sergei bobbed up like a tiny jack-in-the-box, an equally tiny gun in his hand.

Utterly startled, Warren could not suppress a croak of fear. This was the first time, outside of the movies, he had ever seen anybody but a police officer holding a real gun. Olga's reaction was stronger. "Fucking asshole!"

"Shut up!" shouted Sergei. "Both of you." He shoved the gun into the base of her neck and said something that Warren guessed meant "Keep driving." Olga didn't move. Sergei cocked the gun and spoke the same words again. Making an exasperated noise, Olga shifted gear and headed south down Bridgeway. Sergei crouched low so that no one in passing cars could spot the gun angled up behind her. They passed the bus stop in a tense silence.

"What's going on?" Warren managed finally.

From the back Sergei's muffled voice was apologetic. "Excuse me, please, it was never my intention to involve you in this. We have to take a little drive and pick up something. My car was taken from me — "

"Repossessed!"

" — and I need to use Olga's, which by the way I bought for her last year brand new. First I asked her nicely and she wouldn't do it, so now we have to do it this way. Actually, I'm glad you're here because I could use an extra guy to help me." There was nothing the least bit menacing in his voice — not even that absence of menace, beloved of thriller writers, that is supposed to convey the greatest menace of all. Against all reason, Warren found himself relaxing.

"Look," Sergei exclaimed, "look at what we are passing now." They had reached the sharp turn in Bridgeway where an old beige Victorian with ugly brown trim was perched at the end of the bay promenade. "That house — do you know it? It is where Jack London wrote *The Sea Wolf*."

"He was already famous by then," Warren said automatically.

"So?"

"So shrinewise it doesn't count." By this Warren meant that *The Sea Wolf* was the kind of half-brilliant self-conscious abortion writers tended to crank out in the gut-wrenching glare of being world famous. He didn't try to explain the fine points of this subtext to Sergei, but apparently he didn't need to because the Russian said immediately, "You are right, it doesn't count if London rented that house when he was already a wealthy man." He paused. "I hope this question is not too personal, but have you made very much money from your writing career?"

Warren had reached the point in his life where he found the question too personal by half, but the man had a gun, after all. On the spot he calculated mentally the cash return off a lifetime of writing little poems published by little quarterlies. In this venue you didn't get paid as a rule, usually copies or a subscription, but there had been one or two in *The New Yorker*, plus three minuscule book advances from a New York publisher, and wait, don't forget the windfall of the Lannan Prize that one year — "All told," he said to Sergei, "Eighteen, nineteen, call it 20K."

"America!" The noise Sergei made was sympathetic and contemptuous at the same time. "European literati have always made their living strictly from the pen. They are honoured and respected by their countries, and they make piles of money also. In Russia Brodsky's last book of poems sold out in a week — 50,000 copies."

Warren grunted. They were winding up Alexander Avenue now, toward the bridge.

"All Russians love Jack London," Sergei went on. "Also from the same time period Ivan Bunin."

"Bunin is a writer I have never read."

"May I speak frankly? You are not missing much. They always give the Nobel Prize to the second raters. Never the Nabokovs, never the Prousts."

"He won the Nobel Prize?"

"Bunin is why there are so many White Russians in San Francisco."

Warren knew the large ingrown community out in the Sunset district where he had grown up, a dreaming territory demarcated by the gold dome of the Orthodox church on Geary whose inhabitants remained stubbornly, irrevocably, indisputably Russian.

"Very sentimental types, those stateless Harbin Russians. Back in China they all read this famous

13

story by Bunin about a rich American man who dies in Italy, 'The Gentleman from San Francisco.' When Mao kicked them out, everybody went to South America, stayed five years to get their visas, then Mecca at last — San Francisco! Olga is related to a bunch of them."

"If you intellectuals are not too busy with your conversation, maybe Sergei can indicate which way he wants me to go."

"You know which way, Olga. Don't play games." To Warren he said, "She's got a PhD in comparative literature but she was raised American, and that means — no offense, please — she herself is not a real intellectual."

To this Olga made no response. She turned off on a side road just before the entrance to Highway 101 and the Golden Gate. Warren recognised it as the exit to the Fort Cronkhite tunnel. Suddenly Olga braked the Mercedes. A small crowd of people was assembled at the tunnel's mouth. There were cars parked along the road, a sound truck, people setting up lights. Sergei prairie-dogged from the back seat. "What's going on?"

A dim memory from the last arts council newsletter, not a document he scanned with fierce attention, came to Warren. "It's the tunnel singer." With a substantially bigger turnout than his own, he noted reflexively.

"Olga, turn around please and go the other way." Grinding the gears, Olga backed up the Mercedes, drove under the freeway, then turned up the road that hugged the dark basaltic cliffs overlooking the Golden Gate. The red towers of the bridge poked up through the now evenly distributed carpet of fog; beyond rose the gleaming white city of San Francisco. Warren checked his watch: 8:30 and still daylight on this long summer night.

The voice came from the back seat. "Tell me what is tunnel singing."

Warren tried to explain. "A kind of avant-garde performance piece. They project their voices inside tunnels or wherever."

Sergei considered. "The Germans have a good word for that. *Unseriös.* It means narcissistic bullshit by egomaniac losers." Encouraged by Warren's little smile, he went on. "Am I right or not? Performance artists! Who wants to hear about their boring pathetic lives?"

Given the situation, Sergei's outrage seemed disproportionate. Nonetheless Warren felt himself warming to the Russian. He could always spot an authentic aesthetic perspective, the kind that, whether you agreed with it or not, took years of serious reflection to construct. He felt the beginnings of respect and only wished Sergei would put down the gun.

They wound up the narrow Headlands road past the sad archaeology of abandoned bunkers that dotted the edges of the cliffs. A military installation since before the Civil War right through to Vietnam, this whole deserted stretch of coast gave off the melancholy air of preparation never followed by use, an old maiden finally consigned to the convent. Where the two-way road ended, Olga guided the big car down a narrow single lane. On this road there was absolutely no swerve room; heart-stopping

15

dropoffs loomed on either side. Sergei and Warren gasped in unison when she dodged a pair of crested California quail that darted in front of the car, but Olga did not falter. At the base of the ridge, she pulled the car safely into the parking lot at the Point Bonita lighthouse trailhead. The lighthouse itself was hidden by a pillar of rock.

Warren stepped out immediately and stretched his arms; nervous tension had knotted his muscles. Sergei guided them away from the car down a small rough dirt trail. A sign warned: "Dangerous Cliffs and Surf." They descended steeply toward the first of three tiny beaches scalloped out of the steep cliffs on the ocean side of the Gate. Olga tripped in her sandals and muttered, then pushed Sergei away when he tried to take her arm. "Oh, she used to *love* me," Sergei sang the Stones riff to Warren: "But it's *all-over-now*."

Warren slipped, too. "Where are we going?"

"A little dropbox where my friends are making a delivery."

Was it drugs? From Prohibition days until very recently, when its lagoon began silting in, the little town of Bolinas just up the coast had been the main dropbox for everything from liquor to marijuana to the harder stuff. It hadn't occurred to Warren that anyone would do that here at the Gate, where weather and surf conditions were far more severe.

By the time they reached the first beach the air was dark and cold. Streams of white foam ran up and back the tilted surface of the grey sand. A small flock of pelicans floated just beyond the shorebreak. As they stood looking at the empty ocean, Olga made a sharp exclamation in Russian.

"This is exactly the right time, exactly the right place," Sergei replied in English, with a polite motion toward Warren that indicated it was rude to exclude him from the conversation in such a primitive way.

"So where are they? And how did they expect you to get back out the trail, with the tide coming in?" The long yellow streamers of foam were indeed gaining ground, forcing them up toward the cliff face. Here Sergei motioned Warren and Olga into a small cave barely high enough to stand upright in. It was good to get out of the cold, but Warren felt seriously claustrophobic. The cave's pitted walls stank of kelp.

"What is it, a boat you're waiting for?"

"Yes," Sergei said.

"The boat's not coming," Olga said to Warren. "I told him. It's a setup."

Warren pointed through the growing dusk. "Look, Sergei. The water's already past our trailhead."

"Don't be so impatient."

Olga made a noise. Warren saw his chance and snatched her purse. He groped inside and took out the cell phone. "I'm calling the Coast Guard."

Sergei waved the gun in his face. "No, you aren't."

"Are you nuts? Do you want to drown?"

Sergei looked at the advancing water and lowered the gun. "Let's get some help, okay. But no authorities. Don't you have any friends?"

"I guess that means you don't." Warren thought

a moment, then dialled. "Hey?" The lone word issuing from the tiny receiver was embedded in an oceanic roar. But it was noise from the other end, not the surf already swirling into the cave.

"Mack, it's Warren. Where are you?"

"The 2 A.M. Club." More crony than friend, truth be told, Mack patronised the only surviving redneck bar in Mill Valley.

"I can barely hear you. Listen, I'm in kind of a spot here."

"Yeah?"

"I'm on a beach outside the Gate with a couple of people. The tide's coming in pretty hard. How quick can you get back to your dock?"

A pause. "High tide's not till 3:45 a.m."

"High tide's here in ten minutes. Can you bring the Whaler around? There's some spare change in it for you." He directed a meaningful look at Sergei, who shrugged. Warren couldn't believe his own cool behaviour in this life-threatening situation; most days even the slightest departure from his solitary ascetic routine was sufficient to send him into hysterical rage and/or panic. "Looks pretty flat out there. You shouldn't have any problem."

Another silence, a long one. He heard Mack take a final gulp of beer and set the glass down. Then: "Where are you exactly?"

Warren felt a rush of relief. "You know that little beach below Point Bonita? We're right around the bend, southern side."

"Bonita Cove. There's three beaches, but I'll spot you. Be about an hour."

An icy surge curled around Warren's Nikes.

"Hurry, for Christ's sake!" Mack grunted and hung up.

With his free hand Sergei twitched the phone away and stuck it in his own jacket pocket. "Who's your friend?"

"Private detective. Lives on his boat over in Sausalito."

"A private *dick*?" Sergei was delighted. "Far out!" Though admirably fluent, he seemed to have learned all his slang from American records of the 1970s. "My favourite literary detective is from San Francisco. You know Dashiell Hammett, of course? The continental op?"

"Of course." Sentence for sentence Warren preferred the laureate of the southland, Raymond Chandler, but did not feel moved to say so.

"What's that story, you know, where this hooker starts telling the continental op how she had this wonderful childhood, then she says this great line? She says her parents thought she was 'the original Miss Jesus.'" Sergei laughed uproariously. "That's Olga all over."

"So now you're comparing me to a whore?"

"No, Olga, I mean that your aunt and uncle thought —"

A rogue wave hit them all at knee level. Warren lost his balance and had to hold onto the slippery surface of the cave wall to keep from being sucked out with the surge. They were soaked now. "What if his friend's car breaks down?" Olga demanded. "What if his boat breaks down?"

"Then he will call the Coast Guard. Relax."

"How's he going to see us down here? We should

19

climb up on the cliff."

"If we do that, it'll be harder to get into the boat," Warren said. "It's better to wait and let him throw us some ropes."

Olga moved to the mouth of the cave. "Let's get up on that rock at the end of the beach, then." She took off her sandals and, showing a nice athleticism, raced the breakers to a sizeable guano-stained rock that separated this beach from the next one over. The two men followed, scrambling up the rock after her until they were about fifteen feet over the water line. It was cold and exposed here, but it felt a lot safer to Warren than the cave.

A three-quarters moon had climbed over the Headlands ridge. Behind the rock rose the arches of the great lit-up bridge; the muted roar of traffic carried over the water like the buzz of a single giant bee. From his own little ledge Warren looked up at the two Russians and in a sudden flash saw their mutual predicament for what it was. A Zazaloff formation, minus the bonhomie and plus unacceptable risk.

Perched on the outcropping above him like an oversized gull, Sergei said: "Now is a good time to discuss your poem 'Wild California.'"

"Sergei, don't be so ridiculous."

"No, Olga, this is good, it takes our mind off things, and besides I want to. Now, Warren — may I call you that?"

"By all means."

"What I want to know is where are these stuffed animals you talk about, these grizzly bears and mountain lions and buffalo — in some kind of amusement park?"

"It's an exhibit," Olga interrupted. "In a museum in Golden Gate Park."

Warren looked at her. "I'm surprised you know about that." Embedded in the poem's language matrix, a layered stratigraphy of styles (the only thing the poem was "about," of course), was an ironic little idea that the wildness of the West, California particularly, had ossified into these still-life *tableaux vivantes* — "Tule Marsh," "Early Sierra Winter," and the like — that were already corny when they were first installed at the turn of the previous century. Yet people never stopped loving the old dioramas; every time the Academy of Sciences tried to ditch them in favour of trendy multimedia installations there was a huge outcry.

A stray breaker dunked cold seawater on Warren's head. He thought of "Between the Tides," with its frozen plastic surf, stuffed seagulls and seals, and started to laugh.

"What's so funny?" Olga demanded. He shook his head.

"Tell me, Warren," Sergei said abruptly. "What is your single greatest regret?"

"*My* greatest regret?" Warren repeated incredulously. "How about yours?"

"Oh, that is easy. That I didn't become a poet like you. That's what I *really* wanted. My older sister back in Moscow is a physicist, my father is a mathematician. Very smart guys, right? Both told me I was no good. A lousy poet. So then I thought, okay, critic, professor. Those who can't, teach. But I also had this little flair, this talent — "

"For bullshit," said Olga.

"For business, and I had this chance to come here, to America, and before I knew it — "

"The doors had closed behind you."

"That is precisely what happened. So — your turn."

Warren hedged. "How do I pick just one?"

"For me, because you're a poet, it's hard to imagine you can have any regrets at all."

Out in the channel a silent vision was moving swiftly toward the mouth of the Gate. It was a huge freighter, black with a flash of red at the waterline, the name *P&O Nedlloyd* emblazoned on its smokestack. Lit up like a ferris wheel, the ship steamed boldly into the night.

Warren said, "I'm sorry I never jumped on one of those freighters and sailed over the horizon." To his surprise he realised that he meant it. Back in the days before the Port of Oakland won the shipping wars, freighters used to berth at a pier on the Embarcadero a few hundred feet below his kitchen window on Telegraph Hill. At night, lights blazing, they looked unbearably romantic. Just the sight of them excited him and made him mad with grief at the same time. "I'm sorry I stayed stuck here inside my tiny life, writing tiny words in my tiny room. There was another life, a better life, waiting for me out there."

"You missed the boat."

"Yes."

"But what if you had caught it? Gone for a little trip? So what?"

"Something would have happened. I'd be different."

"Shut up!" Olga hissed. "I hear something!" They all listened. Warren couldn't hear anything, but a few minutes later a fifteen-foot Boston Whaler came put-putting around the bend, a beacon light at the bow sweeping the water. He stood up cautiously on the rock and waved his arms. "Mack! Over here!"

The Whaler pulled alongside a flat outcropping at the base of the great rock. "Hey, Warren." Mack was a tall, lanky man with faded brown hair sticking out from his baseball cap and a faint Okie accent.

Warren decided to skip the introductions. He held the bow steady while Olga and Sergei climbed aboard. Then he jumped in himself and used an oar to push off from the rock.

Mack revved the motor and spun the boat into open sea. Once they were safely out of the breaker line, he looked from Warren to Sergei and Olga. "Where to, kids?"

"Can you get us to the beach at Fort Cronkhite?" Warren said. "Our car's at the lighthouse parking lot."

"Yep, should be okay. It'll be flat around the Potato Patch." The Potato Patch was a treacherous shoal of white froth just north of Point Bonita and the site of many shipwrecks in the old days. Keeping well clear of the cliffs, Mack guided the boat past the looming bulk of Point Bonita and its winking light and made his approach toward the mouth of the large valley around the bend. He cut the motor as the Whaler hit the surf line. Once they were past the breakers, Warren jumped out and dragged the boat in till it touched bottom. "Get out," he said to Olga and Sergei, and they both jumped over the side,

Olga stifling an exclamation as her legs hit the freezing water. Sergei, already on shore, was reaching into his pants pocket. He tossed a large, neatly rubber-banded wad of money back into the boat.

Mack looked at the bills where they floated in the bilgewater. "Later," he said to Warren. He cranked up the engine and pulled the Whaler away from the beach, leaving a feathery white wake like a duck's back in the black ocean water.

They walked up the empty road along a brackish-water lagoon, moving fast to stay warm. Warren guessed it would take them thirty minutes to climb the hill to the parking lot. "If I may return to our discussion about your poem," Sergei said, his breath coming out in little puffs of moisture, "I must respectfully say I don't agree. Your state was, is, and always will be wild! You still have grizzly bears. And think of the natural disasters — the earthquakes, the floods, the mudslides. And over there — " he gestured beyond the dark wall of the valley toward the hidden lights of the city.

"Give me a break," Warren interrupted. He could guess what was coming: Twain, Harte, Bierce, and the Barbary Coast. "It's a yuppie Victorian theme park. A place to film car chase movies." Above them in the moonlight loomed the ruin Warren had always mentally labelled the Max Ernst Petrified City Bunker.

"You are being too hard, my friend. You don't appreciate what you've got. I went over to the university in Berkeley, to their rare book library, and I asked to see the letters of Ambrose Bierce and they brought them out to me, in the reading room! Just imagine, I touched Ambrose Bierce's last letter from

Mexico, dated 1913, with my own hands!" Sergei's pale blue eyes gleamed. "In Russia, these days, that would never happen. It would just get stolen."

They were now passing, a sign informed them, the "historic Nike missile site," lovingly maintained, Warren knew, by the nephew of a famous war hero and a crew of zealots. The original outbuildings had been impeccably restored and metal doors in the earth concealed a real (though disarmed) Nike missile, painted a gleaming white and black. Sergei stopped in his tracks next to the wire fence. "Oh man, the irony. You have no idea."

"The irony?"

"Back in the sixties and seventies all us ordinary Russian folk were shitting in our pants because we knew you'd wipe the floor with us if there was a war. You just *needed* to think we were strong, man!"

Up the road the Mercedes sat in the trailside parking lot. Its driver's side door hung open, casting a pool of light on the dirt. A figure was hunched over the steering wheel. "Hey, bastard!" shrieked Olga. "Quit stealing my car!" The man looked up quickly. Then two other men stepped out of a white van parked next to the Mercedes.

"Shut up, Olga! Everybody run!" Sergei hissed. They wheeled and ran back down the road. In the darkness heavy footsteps pounded behind them. A voice boomed out in Russian, followed by a pistol crack. Sergei and Olga came to a quick halt, and Sergei yanked at Warren's coattail. "Stop, stop, or they'll shoot you. Put up your hands."

The three men walked up. The first thing Warren noticed was that amid varying heights and ages, all had sizeable guts. And wore truly horrible rayon jogging suits and cheap running shoes. The leader was a silver-haired patriarch with a deeply lined face. The second, a man in his forties, was short and stout. The third looked barely out of his teens; his premature pouch contrasted strangely with his height and storklike limbs.

Now Sergei was talking fast, a veritable torrent. To Warren's ear spoken Russian sounded like snakes and butter, all sibilants and vowels taking off in one direction, then twisting back into sibilant Ys. The three men listened without expression. Finally the oldest raised his hand. Sergei fell silent immediately. Warren fancied he detected a sort of prodigal son-to-father relation between the young poet turned businessman and this stern, deliberate elder.

The Russians led them back to the parking lot. The middle-aged man snapped his fingers at Olga. Silently she handed over her set of keys. He got in the Mercedes and started the engine while the tall young man taped Sergei's hands together in front of him with duct tape. As the elder climbed in the passenger seat in front, the young man motioned them into the back of the van and locked them inside.

As soon as the doors shut behind them, Olga began kicking Sergei in the shins. "Bastard, silly shit! You stole their money!"

Holding up his taped hands against her blows, Sergei said to Warren, "I *invested* it! If the company hadn't tanked, I would have made a tenfold profit! Tenfold!"

"Fucking dotcom bullshit!" Olga wiped her hair off her forehead and turned to Warren. "He had to be the big shot. So he used their money to play Ponzi games. Now we all get to pay for it. Asshole!"

Warren wasn't listening. Gripped by an ancient memory, he was in the middle of his own very private nervous breakdown. He could feel sweat breaking out under the seawater that still dripped from his brow. From just such a white van as this, back in the seventies, the infamous "Zebra" killers had terrorised the city, committing random murders. A block away from his house they had beheaded a woman. I'm going to die, he thought.

"Warren!" Sergei said.

Reluctantly he looked up. "Listen to me." For once Sergei sounded serious. As well he might. "Don't worry, you will both be okay. Believe me."

"Believe you?" Olga spat in his face. "Nobody believes you." Sergei hunched over awkwardly, trying to wipe the spittle off on the shoulder of his suede jacket.

The van was travelling at an ominously slow, deliberate speed. Warren had been fairly sure he knew when they were still on the curvy Headlands road, then a brief acceleration onto Highway 101 uphill, that would be north, then they were off the freeway again — would it be Spencer, winding back down into Sausalito? For some reason this route seemed more frightening to him than speeding off into the country. A number of sharp turns followed, then the van stopped. There was the sound of the front door opening, followed by steps around the side of the van. Warren's chest tightened. The back door opened abruptly on the tall young man. He said something in Russian and motioned to Olga, who beckoned to Warren. "Get out." He followed her and stepped out of the van in front of a dark bungalow on a hillside street lined with date palms.

"This is my house," Olga said. "We're okay." The relief in her voice was palpable. Her Mercedes pulled up behind the van and the other young Russian got out of it. He tossed the keys in the gutter and climbed in the driver's side of the van.

"Sergei, come," Olga motioned. Still crouched behind the big man at the back door, Sergei shook his head. She turned to the young man, her voice rising. "What's going on?" The passenger door opened and the older man walked around the side of the van. He said something briefly to Olga. A moment passed, then she threw herself against his chest, screaming and beating her fists. The impassive elder silently absorbed her blows. The young man made a motion as if to pull her away, but the old man waved his hand.

"*Tikah*, Olga." Sergei's voice came from the van. She stopped and backed away. The old man turned and went back around the van as the young man climbed in the back with Sergei. Just then Warren caught a glimpse of Sergei's face framed over the young man's bulky shoulder. Warren searched for words to describe that expression and found he had none. Then the young Russian turned around, pushed Sergei back, and slammed the doors shut. The headlights winked on and the van pulled away down the residential street.

He stood in the empty street next to Olga for several minutes before he noticed that her body was shaking. She was crying without making a sound.

At last she said a word, like an exhalation.

"*Seryozha.*"

After a moment Warren said, "What will they do to him?"

She had composed herself. "Who knows?"

"Why did they even let us go? We're witnesses."

Olga turned to face him and Warren marvelled once more at her endless reservoir of contempt. "Oh, *you'll* be okay, don't worry. They have no idea who you are."

"And of course *you* won't tell them if they catch up with you," he said angrily.

She bent down to pick up the keys from the gutter. "Get in the car. I'll take you to your bus."

"The buses stopped running hours ago. I'll show you where to drop me off."

In a weird reprise of their first trip, they drove down the hill, passing the library in silence. Warren had her stop first at the entrance to Kappas Marina. She waited with the motor running while he walked over to the pay phone outside the closed convenience market and dialled 911. When the operator answered, he said: "I want to report a kidnapping." Warren spelled Sergei's name, described the white van, gave its license number, and hung up. Then he walked back to the car. "I wouldn't go back to your house if I were you," he said.

"There's no need to be so worried. He made a deal. That's why we're still walking around."

"A deal?"

"Here's your dock." She pulled up at the Kappas entrance and Warren got out. "What kind of deal?" But the Mercedes' wheels were already rolling; he was barely able to close the door behind him as the car roared off. The big car's taillights blinked once at the parking lot exit before it pulled out onto the road and disappeared.

Warren tiptoed out the dock to Mack's berth. The *Easy*, a twenty-nine-foot Columbia, sat dark and silent. Tripping over ropes, gas canisters, and other assorted junk strewn across the dock, he climbed on board. He knocked softly on the spotty, bubble-filled varnish on the wooden hatch. "Mack!" he hissed.

The hatch slid open. Warren found himself looking down the narrow iron barrel of an enormous Colt. A strangled cry that was nearly, but not quite, a laugh burst from his lips. The second time tonight.

Mack lowered the gun. "Now what?"

Warren waited for his heart to stop thumping. Mack had had his own share of run-ins, of course, even though eighty-five percent of his business consisted of paranoid wives who hired him to find out if their husbands were unfaithful. But Warren doubted that Mack had ever been close to anything like tonight's action. Not that he knew one quarter of it, or ever would. For a quiet guy, Mack was notorious for his big, indiscreet mouth after a drink or three — rather a fatal flaw in his line of work, which was maybe why there never was much of it.

"What happened to those cute friends of yours?"

"Gone their merry way. Can I crash on your deck?"

There was a pause. "Tell you what," Mack said finally, looking out at the water. "The wind's picking up. Let's sail you home. I got a pal at the St. Francis who'll let me tie up in his berth. C'mon, it'll be a gas. Unless you've had enough of the water for one evening."

Warren reflected. He still felt deeply shaken. Maybe this would help him come to terms with what had happened. "Sure."

Mack jumped out of the hatch into the cockpit and was already fiddling with the ropes. "Hey, nothing beats night sailing on the bay."

Warren settled himself in the snug cockpit, leaving all the work to Mack, who had his little ketch rigged single-sailor. In minutes they were out in open water, passing the dark silent bulk of Angel Island. Now was the time, he told himself, for an urgent private review of how tonight's episode impacted his future. Would he have to move, unlist his phone, spend the rest of his days feeling like a walking target every time he gave a reading? Deal or no deal, not for a minute did he buy Olga's assurances that no one would come after him. In one short evening the joke had morphed into a sinister new version: The poet goes to the public library to give a reading and finds only one man in the audience. Halfway through, the man gets up and shoots the poet. *Then* the police come and arrest him.

But in the great silence here at the middle of the San Francisco Bay, broken only by the sensuous lapping sound of the wooden boat's keel dipping up and down through the waves, Warren relaxed in spite of himself and found himself thinking — to his own astonishment — about Jack London's stories of the oyster pirates who plied the bay back in the days people like Sergei felt such nostalgia for. Truth be told, Warren had loved those tales as a teenager.

London was already exaggerating his own he-man role, of course — everybody forgot this was the guy Hemingway copied — but still it was fun to read, this early stuff.

What on earth had got him going on that? Warren had the oddest feeling that his two Russian acquaintances of this evening were still with him, even *in* him. He had never been intimate with Olga, yet that hateful voice had somehow entered his blood like a virus, become part of him. From now on, he somehow knew with great certainty, it would rise out of nowhere to offer mocking commentary on his daily failings. As for Sergei — he had a sudden mad vision of an arm hooked over the stern and the dripping Russian hauling himself into the boat, shamelessly reinserting himself in Warren's life like the sea captain's stowaway in that Conrad story (an allusion Sergei himself would have been the first to identify). But in a way Sergei had already done this. Warren couldn't get the Russian, and the Russian's literary obsessions (which had proved rather conventional after all), out of his head. What had been done to Sergei, what was being done to him even as Warren sat safely in the cockpit of his friend's boat?

His last sight of the Russian came to him like a gentle grace note. Meeting the simple kindness in Sergei's eyes in the back of the van, he felt he had been permanently touched, altered. Would an American look like that, in the same situation? Some Americans might, he realised. It took a history of major persecution — Warren could almost hear Sergei pointing out that the word *slave* derived from *slav* — to put anything but stark terror on your face at that moment. Under those desperate conditions, did people — some people — discover ways of expressing their humanity that were completely out of reach for their luckier, more sheltered brethren?

Here Warren's cynicism intervened. Wasn't Sergei's accumulated bad karma the direct result of trying to *be* American? His chosen profession, the madness that enveloped Russia now, was so very entrepreneurial, so very lawless, so very American.

Overwhelmed by the forbidden urge to smoke, he reached instinctively for his pocket and his hand brushed against plastic. With a deep shame that seemed to rise all the way from the soles of his feet, he realised that the button with its grotesque logo had been prominently displayed on his chest throughout the night's events. He unfastened the button and tossed it quickly overboard, where it hit the water with a gentle chonk and disappeared. The wrong person had been wearing it, of course.

Mack's voice broke through his thoughts. "Are you going to tell me what this was all about?"

Warren grunted. "Better you don't know." Now they were approaching the abandoned docks and warehouses under Telegraph Hill and he stood up abruptly. "Drop me off here."

"The St. Francis is just around the bend."

"This is fine."

"As you wish."

The *Easy*'s bow bumped against the pilings of an enormous empty pier, and they both lurched forward in the cockpit. Mack cut the engine and Warren looked up.

The old dock loomed a good twenty feet over the

boat. The tar-soaked piling nearest him had a vertical row of spikes spaced at regular intervals. The spikes were rusty orange, but they looked sturdy. Warren gripped the highest one he could reach, pulled himself over the railing and planted his left foot on another spike level with the deck. As the boat drifted away from the pilings, he quickly hoisted his other leg over the railing.

"Know where we are?" he called across the strip of streetlight reflections between the pier and the *Easy*.

Mack restarted the engine. "Embarcadero at Battery."

"Wrong. It's the Barbary Coast. The original Barbary Coast."

Mack laughed ironically. He knew how much Warren hated local colour.

"And Mack? Keep tonight to yourself, okay?" A useless request, but he had to make it.

"Sure thing." Mack's voice floated insincerely over the water. The gap widened very quickly as the *Easy* motored into the night.

He'd been counting on Mack to stick around until he was sure he could make it safely up to the dock. Now, it seemed, he was committed to the piling. Warren gripped the spikes. To the east a thin band of light rimmed the hills. Hands bright with rust, he began to climb.

The Road to Te Nono

The road to Te Nono is long and full of unexpected sights. From Wellington, that city of melancholy nineteenth-century public buildings at the bottom of the world, the motorway winds north through the Hutt Valley between steep cliffs covered with yellow broom, then veers inland over a pleasant stretch of rolling hills terraced with hundreds of ancient criss-crossing sheep trails, whereon the sheep themselves assemble in stately rows, an eternal frozen tableau. To the west rise the sharply etched folds of a little mountain range, to the east the Tasman Sea. Dotted promisingly with tree ferns, this countryside is green as the tropics but also very cold, as if locked in a permanent false spring.

I got off the Road Services bus at Palmerston North, a fair-sized provincial farming city. The bus stop abutted a modest square dominated by a large, ugly clock tower under which an exhibition of Highland dancing seemed to be taking place. Noontime crowds thronged the promenade. I stood for a moment with my overnight bag taking them all in, this tough, seedy little nation of do-it-yourselfers

— the big florid men in shorts and knee socks, the children in school uniform going home for lunch, the women in flowered frocks pushing babies in sheepskin-lined prams. The square was ringed with a confusing array of small shops, many of which were clones of each other — greengrocers, chemists, butchers, "gift boutiques" with hideous ornaments for sale, television repair stores. Each boasted its own modest, tightly lettered sign swinging in front, so that all you saw in any direction was an endless replication of pinched typefaces, row upon row mirrored into infinity. High over the rooftops a bronze kiwi revolved like an icon on a metal staff.

I was to meet Barry in a coffee-house called Sasa's, near the square, he had said on the phone, so I began searching for something resembling the San Francisco variety in this unlikely setting. He hadn't said *coffee-house*, in fact; he had used some other, similar word to describe it. After a few false starts down streets that seemed to hold only more little shops with little signs, I recrossed the square — past the flashing kilts, the Martian wail of bagpipes — and wound up in the rundown part of town, where teenage Maori boys clustered in shabby fish and chips shops and Space Invader arcades. In one of these byways of boarded-up storefronts I spotted the sign for Sasa's Coffee Lounge (that was the word) and walked confidently in. It stood to reason, I felt, that somehow, as in Australia, an Italian or two would have found his way to Palmerston North and set up a proper cappuccino bar.

I found myself in a cavernous black-walled room lit by naked pink bulbs screwed into remote sockets on the ceiling. Lawn tables spray-painted white were lined up stiffly against the walls. In the gloomy regions at the rear a tow-headed youth behind the service counter waited without curiosity as my eye scanned the menu on the plastic marquee over his head: savaloys, meat pies, bread-and-butter pikelets, fruit drink (this was likely to be Tang), instant coffee — the standard gut-curdling Kiwi cuisine. I ordered tea, and the boy silently rang up my money. Behind him, posted squarely at the opening to the kitchen, a notice cautioned:

Please do not Ask to use Our conveniences, as Refusal may cause Offence.

I took my tea to a seat near the front, where a bit of watery afternoon light filtered in through the window grillwork. On the sidewall another notice was neatly taped.

Please don't Damage or Take property from this Restaurant. Thank you.

An identical sign hung in the same spot over every other table in the room. On the upper walls posters were tacked side by side in the same rigid symmetry displayed by children or the mentally disturbed. Cheek by jowl with John Lennon and the Irish Rovers were colour pictures of horses and kittens, ads for vinyl house paint and crawler tractors, souvenir tea towels of New Zealand scenes stretched taut and thumbtacked in place. Over the door two Japanese umbrellas opened stiffly to attention. Next to them a straw basket hung at a rakish angle, balanced by an identical one beneath positioned in exactly the opposite direction.

I was sipping my tea when a middle-aged Kiwi in shorts and knee socks burst in the door. The screen, which was badly hung, swung dramatically shut behind him but stopped just short of making contact with the frame, so there was no satisfying slam but only a kind of spectral "whoosh!" The man turned around. It was Barry.

Barry had always been slight of build, but as I hugged him now I could feel not only the ribs down his back but the slackness of the muscles that carried them, as if some vital fluid had been tapped out of his spine. He had shaved off his signature little black beard and moustache, too. Now his face looked younger even while his body felt older, defeated.

We sat down. "Well!" Barry exclaimed. Something in the way that innocent word rolled off his tongue rang a warning bell. "Say again?"

He was puzzled. "Had a good trip, Grace?"

It was the vowels, I realised. "Barry, you can spit out the Weetbix. It's me."

He looked pleased. "Sound like a Kiwi now, do I?"

"I'll say."

We regarded each other warily. "Can't help it, that's the way I talk now." Barry dismissed the topic with a shrug. "What do you think of all this?" He waved his arm, which looked rather spectral trapped in the tidal bore of pink lighting and afternoon sun.

"I think it captures the New Age ethos beautifully."

"New Zealand, I mean. Besides, what's wrong with this place? I thought you'd like it." He sounded defensive. "Quite the lively scene on Saturday night. I always come here when I'm in Palmerston."

I paused a minute, then said, "Wellington's all right. I liked the ride up here. I've only been in the country two weeks, you know."

"You've got a Fulbright, right?" said Barry. "That means you'll be here a year." In the past, fellowships, appointments, and related career issues always had the effect of making him grow wonderfully focused. It was heartening to see the familiar reflex working now, though creakily, like a middle-aged ballerina going *en pointe.*

"I'm only going to be at the Turnbull Library a few months," I said. "After that, I'm off to the Solomons."

A touch of the old condescension appeared in Barry's voice. "You're not still into the Proto-Melanesian Pacific migration stuff, are you?"

I am a linguist, you see. My area of specialty is origins, migrations — where people come from, where they end up. It's all there, in the language. Turn-of-the-century philologists had nothing on me. Old-fashioned anthropologists like Barry weren't interested in culture origins, or culture theory either, for that matter; long ago they had staked their careers on ecological adaptation. But systems theory was no longer hot stuff. It had been not such been hot stuff for such a long time, in fact, that one could predict with dead certainty it would soon be back in fashion again. Barry was actually riding the wave of the future, not the past.

"Yes," I said.

Barry cleared his throat. "Michigan give you tenure?"

"Last year."

He stuck out his hand. "Congratulations." We shook. Then he said, in his odd accent, "It's a fair distance to Te Nono and there's not much to eat at home. What do you say to getting something here?"

I hesitated, thinking of the menu. "How about a Chinese restaurant?" That seemed safe. If the Italians hadn't made it to Palmerston North, surely the Chinese had.

"Wouldn't be open at this hour of day. The food's not bad right here. Had a savaloy yet? Try one."

The thought of those plump, greasy sausages made me wince. In New Zealand the beef was beefier, the milk milkier than an American stomach weaned on watery white fluid and flesh pumped full of steroids was used to. It was a harder adjustment to make than you might think. "Go ahead and get something for yourself, Barry. I had a big lunch."

"Oh, never mind." There was disappointment in Barry's voice, as if I had confirmed something he had suspected all along. He stood up from the table. "It's a long drive. We'd best get started."

When Barry and I were in the car and safely off down a ribbon-narrow highway bordered with green fields, I ventured to ask what had not seemed politic to bring up during our discussion of tenure back at Sasa's.

Barry paused. "For the time being the Department of Maori Affairs is buying my groceries," he said.

He did not take it any further. From my unfamiliar lefthand passenger side I looked out the window. We were heading from the inland flats back toward the coast. A vast cloud shadow lay over the North Island. Behind us the afternoon sun lit up the little green mountain range in a supernal glow. By contrast, the advancing plate of ocean looked a sickly pale blue — *watery* blue, I almost said. It did not possess the radiant virile colours of the land. The Tasman Sea. As people here were fond of telling me, there was nothing but it between this coast and Antarctica.

Te Nono was a motley collection of houses, post office, small general store or "dairy," and Maori meeting house huddled in the scrub just off the beach — and a wild and windswept beach it was, gusting sand in billows as we arrived just before sundown, metallic breakers crashing on the shore. At one end of the beach was a jumbled rockslide; from it a small series of sad little grassy hillocks stretched up the coast in a haze of salt spray.

Without warning Barry pulled the car into a dirt driveway right off the main road. Behind a barrier of hedges we rocked onto the unkempt lawn of an old house with wooden paint-flecked posts holding up the small veranda, curlicue wooden "lace" at the top, and a corrugated tin roof painted green. "Rui!" Barry called, before he was even out of the car.

A twelve-year-old girl in plaid skirt and jumper appeared in the doorway as Barry was taking my bag from the back seat. "Meet Grace, my friend from America," he said.

Rui had pale skin, blue eyes, and close-cropped jet

black hair. She smiled at me in a friendly, guarded way. To Barry she said, "I've got to go over to Mere's straightaway, Dad."

"They've got your tea for you, have they?"

"Yes." She looked impatiently at the ground.

Barry gave her shoulder an affectionate pat. "Very well, then. Off you go."

Rui ran down the steps and started up the road in a single-minded way, head down as if deep in thought. To be a New Zealand Maori with a bookish American Jewish father, I thought, must set you rather apart. But did she get her blue eyes from her Jewish ancestors or her Maori ones? As Barry guided me into a modest living room appointed with the New Zealand regulation overstuffed furniture, gas heater, and white gauze curtains, I said: "I'll bet Rui is good in school."

"Good?" said Barry proudly. "She's tops in all her subjects. Next year I'm sending her down to boarding school in Wellington. Her mother and her relatives don't want me to, of course. You're not supposed to put yourself too much above everybody else here, you know. Cultural thing. That's Rui's mother." He pointed to a monograph on the mantel. The eyes of a startlingly beautiful Maori woman stared back at me out of a cheap metal frame. "Lives down in Paekak — that's Paekakariki — with the licensee of the local hotel. They've got two little boys now. Poor old Rui feels a bit left out, stuck up here with me. Here, have a look. The school paper just printed some of her poetry."

He thrust a stapled sheaf of papers in my hand, folded over to a page toward the end.

42

"Shells at Sunset" by Rui Goldberg

Walking the beach
My foot strikes a beautiful coloured object.
It is all that is left of a living creature.
Body here, spirit gone.
An empty shell.

Barry took the paper out of my hands just as abruptly. "Rui has leukemia," he said. "She went through the most bloody awful treatment now. We just hope for the best. The doctors say it's all blown over, but it knocked the child right out of her, poor little thing. Good, though, isn't it?"

I nodded.

"We were going back to the States last year, me and Rui. With a penny and a prayer — I have all the job prospects of a felon there. But then *this* happened, and I put the trip off. Now I've given it up altogether. Too strange for Rui." He sighed. "It's like living at the bottom of a well down here. You read about America, the same old bullshit, and it starts to sound like Mars. So I'm sending Rui to this girls' school in Wellington instead. It's tops, the prime minister's daughter went there. At least Rui'll have a chance to be something in her own country."

He looked restlessly out the window, though it was dark now and there was nothing to see. "When were you last in the U.S., Barry?" I asked.

"Seven years ago, when my father died.' He smiled. "I was still thinking like an American then, so it didn't seem so weird. Now I reckon I'd be just as out of place as Rui."

"Even in Berkeley?"

His face lit up briefly. "One always keeps one's citizenship there, doesn't one? Hang on, let me fix you some tea."

I was about to say I didn't want any more tea when I realised Barry meant dinner. His voice trailed through the doorway. "Warned you we should have eaten in Palmerston North. All there is is beans on toast."

He had been looking forward to eating out in the big city, of course. I got up to join him in the kitchen. Barry's kitchen boasted a 1950s Frigidaire, a gas stove, and the ubiquitous electric jug. Over the kitchen table hung a Snoopy poster and a painted wooden plaque of a German shepherd. Something in the relentless positioning of these pictures seemed strangely familiar. Then I remembered Sasa's Lounge. A far cry from Tibetan temple hangings and posters of Huey Newton in the rattan chair, the artifacts I had last seen surrounding Barry a couple of lifetimes before. He had always let his girlfriends fix up those places, I recalled. What I now saw must be Rui's handiwork.

"Ever keep up with our mutual friends?" I asked him.

"Used to. Gave it up. All those anthropology conferences people go to in Tokyo, Manila, Sydney — you have to spend a lot of extra money to stop off in little old En Zed. Plus I live way down here, not close to Auckland at all. Te Nono's definitely off the touring circuit. But you must see those folks all the time, eh? Triple A meetings, that sort of thing?"

"No," I said. "Hardly any of our old crowd's still

44

in anthro. I only see them when I go back to Berkeley. Everyone still goes back there. Kind of amazing, after fifteen years."

Barry dumped a can of Wattie's beans into a saucepan and gave them a professional stir. "So you finished up at Berkeley, spent two years in Indonesia, then Michigan, now here, then the Solomons?"

"I seem to pull up stakes every couple of years," I said. "Even since I got on at Michigan I've hardly spent more than nine months at a time there."

"How I envy you, junketing around the world like that."

"The thrill is gone. I don't know where I belong anymore. I want to settle down, but just to pick a spot now and call it home seems so artificial."

"I've got news for you," Barry said slowly. "You don't get to pick the spot. It picks you."

There was a little silence. Then I said, "You seem to fit in amazingly well here."

"I try."

"What is it you do for the Department of Maori Affairs?"

"I'm involved with the people," he said vaguely. "If you think I sound like a Kiwi, wait till you hear me speak Maori."

He whipped two slices of spongy white bread out of the bread box and stuck them in an antiquated toaster, the kind with chromium wings on each side. "Want to hear the story of how the god Maui fished the North Island out of the sea? Kind of an old chestnut, but the tourists like it."

He launched into a sonorous recitation, punctuating his speech with a certain amount of vigorous gesturing. I knew the story was over when he said suddenly, in English, "That's a bit tame, really. You should hear the naughty tales. Te Nono's a rude word, by the way. All the old ladies giggle about it. Quite the joke in these parts."

"What does it mean?"

Barry smiled into the beanpot. It was the first real trace of humour I had seen him show. "I believe the veil of secrecy around some traditional information ought to be maintained, don't you? Isn't that the enlightened postcolonialist credo?"

We sat down at the bare kitchen table. On each large naked plate a small piece of toast was heaped high with steaming baked beans. A battered tin teapot sat in the middle.

I looked at the repast. "Don't you ever miss hot pastrami sandwiches?"

"Right, you don't go for the local cuisine. Well, Grace, you adapt. You adapt and survive. It's been a long time since I thought about hot pastrami sandwiches, baseball, or art movies." He said it smugly, lighting into his beans on toast.

"What about religion?"

"What about it?"

"How are you raising Rui?"

"Rui's Mum and all her family belong to the Ratana Church, and so does Rui. That's a Maori evangelical sect. I won't try to explain what it's about, too complicated. Ratana was my dissertation topic, did you know that? Too bad I never managed to finish it. Life caught up with me. The real-life Ratanas pushed out the ones on paper. The ones in

46

my head." He laughed, but it was not a hearty sound. "I guess that's what I wanted."

The bad meal was making me cross. "You're supposed to observe your subject, not identify with it," I said. "Barry, you've gone bush."

He chewed carefully before replying. Such was the aging process among all my old friends that now I could see the outline of his skull as he doggedly pursued his methodical mastication. When he finished, he said, "I wouldn't call a wonderful daughter 'going bush.'"

A long silence followed in which we sipped out tea and I decided not to try to make amends. A few years ago I would have handled it differently. My personality was changing, I realised. Did that make me better now, or worse? I realised I didn't much care. That was different, too.

Barry gave an exaggerated stretch in his hard-backed no-nonsense New Zealand kitchen chair. "It's been a long day," he said. "I'm buggered."

I took the cue. "Me, too."

We both got up gratefully. "I'll just show you where you'll sleep tonight. In Rui's room, if that'll do." Taking my bag, he led the way down a narrow hall to a windowless little back room sparsely furnished with cot, dresser, and small desk. Pictures from magazines were scotch-taped to the walls and a worn stuffed panda bear sat on the bed. "Here you are," said Barry. "Conveniences down the hall. I'll just turn on the hottie for you. You know about hotties, don't you?" I did. A hottie was an electric blanket strapped directly to the mattress under the sheet, an ingenious device that was an absolute necessity in the little country's eternally damp climate.

"All set? Right. Pleasant dreams." Barry walked stiffly out the door. Maybe this problem would sort itself out by morning, I thought, undressing quickly in the cold little room and putting on a flannel nightgown. I shut out the light, stretched full length on the narrow bed, and closed my eyes. But sleep did not come.

Back when I knew him Barry was always losing women, and as I was always losing men that made us a kind of uneasy kin. In Berkeley, all this happened. Once we had spent the night together. "Don't do me any favours," Barry had said at the start. You never forget what you think about someone who says a thing like that. I wondered what Barry was thinking about tonight, lying alone in his room at the other end of the house.

Barry was a nervous Chicago intellectual in those days. Coming to graduate school in California was his way of getting out of his head and going native — the first step, if you thought about it, on the way to Te Nono. Along with that went the irony; Barry was nothing if not ironic. Finicky in his personal tastes, he had the rigid, brittle mental set that always shields a most fragile and delicate male sensibility. He needed to dominate intellectually and got extremely cross when he couldn't.

The nature of those times was that they never seemed to end. All the possibilities, waking up on a cool, crisp northern California morning with a new something to learn, a new someone to know. You met somebody — wonderful. You lost them — the end of the world. And so all the boyfriends and girl-friends came and went. Barry hooked up with a Russian woman, a real character named Irina. Irina was a linguist like me. One time she gave a Proto-Indo-European costume party to which you were supposed to come dressed according to your pet theory of where the forebears of Western culture, the Proto-Indo-Europeans, had sprung from. It was all very Berkeley. People came in saris, spacesuits, bearskins. Irina served substances with cognate roots in Proto-Indo-European: mead, honey, and a rather basic brown bread from the Co-op.

What Irina had in abundance was temperament. That fascinated the prim and rational Barry. Also she was Russian, and as Barry's family was German Jewish, they had those cultural ironies to savour as well. That was the big thing then, savouring ironies. Barry and Irina used to sit side by side in the Cafe Mediterraneum sipping cappuccino and reading their favourite authors. A cultural chameleon even then, Barry read Dostoyevsky in honour of his love; Irina preferred Kristeva. Underneath the emotion-alism there was quite a strong pedagogical streak in her nature — more so than in Barry's, as it turned out; Irina now holds the Citizen's Chair at Illinois.

I believe Barry also went with a girl named Sarah, a Midwest radical he lost to the women's movement. Not all of Barry's women left him; he did his share of breaking up. But when Barry cut himself loose from someone, it was always with the implicit assumption that she was about to leave him anyway, so better to get in the first lick and save face. On

49

more than one occasion I had observed him cut his own throat in this manner and lie bleeding on the ground, all in the name of self-defence.

Now, all these years and halfway around the world later, things seemed to have worked out about the same. Immaterial whether Barry left his wife or she left him; the outcome kept Barry's life structurally intact. The only difference I could see was that now he was somebody's father instead of somebody's son. Was that a big difference? Something told me it was, even though I don't have children myself nor seem likely to. In some ways my own story is a lot like Barry's, though lacking the clear-cut pattern — to me, at least. That's why I can understand Barry as I do. Or so I used to think. After all, there were now coffee lounges to take into account. Not to mention the unexpected business about the wonderful daughter. And what, exactly, did "involved with the people" mean? Remembering Barry's old snobbery, I wondered if he had such a lowly job now that he was afraid to tell me. I resolved to ask no further questions.

But what was the truly new factor here? Then it struck me. Except for his coyness about the name of his hometown, Barry was serious. My eyes flew open. That was it. No irony. Barry had turned a corner. A corner I was still on the wrong side of, it seemed. I was dumbstruck. What a discovery to make all alone in a little room on the edge of the Tasman Sea. In the dark I listened for the noise of the ocean. There was none. The wind must have died, too. It occurred to me that I could be anywhere in the world — Ibiza, Dar Es Salaam, the middle of the Gobi Desert. Why here?

Had I finally passed that invisible point in life after which the journey *away from* mysteriously becomes the journey *to*? But of all the places to come to, of all I had ever been in, Te Nono seemed the least justifiable, the most arbitrary. And that was no joke.

"Wake up!" Barry's head appeared halfway through the door. It was morning, the room was light. "Come up front, I want to show you something."

Sleepy-eyed, barefooted, I followed him down the hall to the living room .The cheap electric clock on the mantel said 9:20. How had I slept so long, and where had I been? It was all very disorienting.

Barry squatted by the front window. "Look, I want you to see this. They're calling someone onto the *marae*."

I came to the window. Next door was the little Maori meeting house I had noticed when we arrived the night before. Three Maori men, one in a business suit and the other two in long-sleeved woollen sweaters, stood in front of the carved wooden posts of grimacing ancestors supporting the angled roof. Across the wide expanse of lawn from the greeters a large party of men, women, and children waited near our window, their faces a genetic Rorschach of inter-marriage — now you saw the Maori in them, now the English. It was odd, after all my years in the tropical Pacific, to see those formidable Polynesian bodies jammed into the boxy confines of cold-climate Western dress, enormous uncomfortable-looking leather shoes. New Zealand Maoris always managed to give the impression of being stuck, as if bewitched, in a kind of permanent costume party.

One of the three men cried out. An answering call came back from a woman in the large party across the lawn, a long keening wail that made the hairs on the back of my neck stand up.

"That's the *karanga* she's giving," Barry said. "It's a ritual to make sure visitors don't have war-like intentions before they're let on the *marae*. Just a custom now, but very important protocol. Maoris are big on protocol."

The large group of people was now crossing the lawn to the meeting house, where a number of other people had come out the front door. The visitors seated themselves in a row of chairs facing the meeting house. One of the three men came forward and began a long address in Maori. This speech was answered in kind by one of the visitors. Grey-haired and imposing, the man sounded angry. From his pocket he drew out a sealed envelope, held it aloft and, without pausing in his speech, flung it contemptuously on the ground.

I turned to Barry. "What's going on?"

"They're the visitors, so they're picking up the tab for lunch. That's the money."

"Are they insulted about it, or what?"

He laughed. "No, just doing a bit of rubbishing to get their own back. It's the custom. No one takes offense."

Speeches over, the visitors moved down a long receiving line, embracing and rubbing noses. Laughter carried across the air, Antipodean Cockney accents; they were all speaking English. Even from this distance I caught flashes of brilliant smiles, those glittering eyes of love — the ineffable

Polynesian spirit shining through the flawed human vessel. I sneaked a look over at Barry's crabbed shoulders next to me at the window. So tempting, and so futile, I thought, to attempt to escape one's personal limitations, to hope to possess this *aroha*, this love, by marrying into it. Not the same as bringing it forth inside oneself, making it one's own and then just giving it away, freely squandering it so that it vanishes without a trace as if it had never existed at all, which is the whole point of the thing.

Not that I had managed any of this myself.

Even as I had this thought, Barry stood up and rotated his shoulders unconsciously, as if trying to free them from invisible bonds. "You and I could have gone in as part of the group," he said, "but I didn't want to wake you up. They'll be having quite a spread at lunchtime." He sounded wistful.

"Sorry, it's not like me to sleep so late. Couldn't we go now?"

"No, you have to go in with the group. Why don't you get dressed and we'll have a cup of tea? Then I thought you might like to take a tramp round in the hills. It's beautiful country here."

It sounded like a good plan. My bus to Wellington left at three that afternoon. Back in Rui's room I dressed and zipped up my bag, ready for a quick departure. Efficient comings and goings were my specialty.

"You know," Barry remarked, "You really hurt me last night with that 'going bush' comment."

I was silent a long time. Finally, after we had crossed the narrow highway again and were walking on a badly paved road toward the sea, I said, "I'm sorry." Then I added, and wished I hadn't because it sounded so glib: "Who am I to judge — a rootless cosmopolitan?"

Hands shoved in the pockets of his shorts, Barry walked on. His mouth worked and then he burst out: "No, you're dead right. I'm an outcast here. Know the language better than lots of them, the protocol, the stories — but just because my great-granddad wasn't Tama te Kapua, I'm nothing. Oh, they like me well enough, but it makes no difference. Rui, that's different. She's got a proper genealogy through her Mum."

I didn't know how to respond. Why should the Maoris care about him when it had been Barry's own choice to take up their battle?

Barry reached angrily into his back pocket. "Look," he said, drawing an ancient plastic-covered photo out of his wallet. "That's *my* great-grandfather."

I looked at the tiny sepia print of a nineteenth-century European, no Orthodox Jew certainly, but dressed in formal bourgeois black, a prosperous businessman. "Why does everybody from back then look like all they did was go to funerals?" I asked rhetorically. Our descendants will have an equally stylised image of us — trivial hedonists who frittered away our lives in an endless round of birthday parties, scenic tours, Polaroid-recorded sex. The late great Fun Century.

"Who am I descended from?" Barry went on furiously, ignoring my remark. "The Levis and the Cohens, that's who. And we go back a damn sight farther than the Seven Canoes."

Barry was referring to the Maori equivalent of the Mayflower, the legendary original settlers who came from Tahiti. Spotting the cloud formations over New Zealand from their outriggers in the sea, they had dubbed the country the "Land of the Long White Cloud."

"The Land of the Wrong White Crowd," I said aloud. It was a joke I had heard in Australia.

"Well, exactly. Don't get me started on *that*."

"You ought to revive the old theory that the Polynesians are descended from the Lost Tribes of Israel," I suggested. "Then you'd be related, wouldn't you?"

Barry snorted. "That's why I wanted to take Rui back to the States — so she'd know about that other side of her. *My* side. I'm not religious, no one in my family has been for generations. It's just the whole cultural thing, you know. Not to mention being American. Then she got sick. I can't see yanking her away now. There's a national health service here, see. And it's the best. Just having her monitored in the States would cost a fortune."

"Why don't you come back for a visit while she's in boarding school?"

"No money," said Barry. "Spent it all on her tuition for next year. Couldn't raise the fare to Taihape, let alone New York. I'm stuck."

He stopped and looked at me. "The truth is I love this place, Grace. It just doesn't love me back."

Barry kicked a rock out of his path but otherwise appeared to be calming down. We were on a little hillside now. Below us, on the other side of the road, the land lay under modest cultivation. "Remember that big story when someone sighted UFOs over New Zealand?" he said. "An old Maori woman around here said it had to be her big white cabbages they saw, reflected off the clouds."

Barry laughed with genuine delight, then waved vigorously at someone on the road. It was Rui. She and a little blonde girl walked quickly along the edge of the tarmac, holding hands and singing:

> One man went to mow the meadow,
> Went to mow the meadow,
> With his dog Spot,
> A bottle of pop
> And a sausage roll,
> Went to mow the meadow.

We watched them until they rounded a bend in the road and disappeared.

"You should settle down, Grace," Barry said. "Don't keep putting it off."

I looked at him. "Not someplace like here where you'll never belong," he whispered urgently. "*Home.*"

We stopped in front of an old iron lace gate blocking the road. It was the entrance to a cemetery. Barry opened the gate and we walked into a low-lying stretch of land separated from the beach by high dunes and a row of straggly pine trees. The cemetery had some very old graves, with ornate memorials, and some new ones. On the other side of the dunes came the steady sound of a gentle shore-break.

"I don't know what you'd think of America if you went back, Barry. Honestly I don't. It has all changed there, right under our feet. It doesn't feel like home."

"This cemetery," Barry said as if I had not spoken, "is ninety-five years old. Before that the land belonged to the local tribe for a thousand years or so. The Pakehas — you know, the English colonists — did their usual bit of dirty getting this land made over to them. One of the things they did was to plant a few stiffs to make this section legally a cemetery. After that, everyone started burying their dead here. But most of the Maoris boycott it. Maoris have long memories."

I looked at a tombstone. Mary Elizabeth Higham, Beloved Wife of Thomas Higham, 1867-1931. "Land is really the big issue here, isn't it?"

"Yes," Barry groaned. "It was stolen. They got screwed, they deserve restitution. But it's just a brutal, thankless fight. You get burnt out. After a while all you think is: Marx was right. Property is theft. A hundred years, a thousand years — what's the diff?" He struck a tree trunk with his fist, causing an alien little bird to fly out of it into the sky. Even though the plants and animals in New Zealand looked persistently familiar, most of them I had never seen before — nor was I likely to ever again. This discovery made me strangely anxious.

"Here's what human beings spend their lives worrying about," Barry said. "Whose eel trap, whose *totara* tree? The whole human race is a bunch of bloody thieving peasants and always will be. One set gets in and lords it over the other set, who can't wait for their turn. Christ and Buddha had their work cut out for them, I reckon."

We walked aimlessly between the gravestones. There had been a distant sound of digging and now, at the end of the lot closest to the ocean, we could see a man leaning on a shovel against a mound of dirt. At ground level a shiny blade glinted as it flung earth in the air.

"New tenant moving in?" I inquired.

"That'd be old Mrs. Clyde, from Plymouth," Barry said promptly — trust an anthropologist to keep up with the latest gossip.

We wandered over to where the workman stood. He was an older man, large and heavyset, in woollen work jersey, shorts and knee socks, whose freckles, dainty complexion, and enormous chin marked him as a true son of the British Isles. The English New Zealanders all looked alike to me, less differentiated in their features than the Maoris.

The workman disdained to look up as we approached. But it now became clear that something was terribly wrong with the new grave. Instead of a neatly sized oblong, an untidy circular cavity some twelve feet in diameter gaped before us. At the bottom of this ragged hole, which I had first mistaken for a garbage pit, another worker stood ankle deep in water, doggedly hacking at the caving sides in a vain attempt to straighten them. But with every shovelful more dirt collapsed and ran into the pit.

I stood back as Barry walked gingerly around the volatile rim to the other side."What's going on?" he asked. The worker on top paused, taking in the foreign accent. Though Barry sounded like a Kiwi to me, to them he was very much the Yank. Poor Barry.

"Spring tide," the man said finally. "Goes right under the ground here. Never seen it this bad."

We stared at the open grave. Imperceptibly at first, then in a steady stream, dirt cascaded down the sides, with new fissures constantly opening up in the bare ground a few inches away from the edge.

"If the City Council had planted the grass here like they bloody said they would, this wouldn't be happening," he added bitterly.

Just as he said this, a big chunk of dirt dropped off the far end of the hole, now some fifteen feet across and actively growing. The pool of water at the bottom was deepening, too.

"Shit," said Barry, and I backed away on my side.

"It's like quicksand," the man in the hole spoke for the first time. He had a high tenor voice and sounded excited. "If I try to get out of here, I'll bring the lot down."

We all looked down at the man in the hole. Hard luck for him. Barry came back around to my side of the pit. "Very Proto," I said to him. It was an old joke of ours. He didn't smile, and I couldn't read the expression on his face. "That's where I'll go," he said. "In *their* ground." I was puzzled. Did he mean Maori ground, Pakeha ground, Gentile ground, or simple foreign ground? Not his ground, it seemed clear, whatever the category.

"Yars," said the older gravedigger imperturbably. "You could fit a whole battalion in this one, I reckon."

"Bugger this, I'm getting out," the man in the hole said suddenly. He scrambled up the far side, tripping off an avalanche of earth. Finally, grinning sheepishly, he stood on top, but only after another two-foot section had collapsed.

"No worries," said the bigger man. "Tide'll be down by tomorrow morning. We'll come back early and shape it out proper."

"Right," said his mate. "At the slant instead of straight up and down." He slung the shovel over his shoulder and they walked quickly away.

I looked down at the pond of water collected in the bottom of the hole. The Tasman Sea. For some reason it made me think of Ben, an old friend from Berkeley. Barry had known him, too. A quiet guy, Ben, not much ambition. I left him for a love that didn't amount to much more, in the end. Left him to rot. That happened back in those years I've spoken of. Precious years, and they're gone now.

I turned to Barry but he was gone, too. Halfway across the cemetery and, by the look of him, in no mood to linger. So I left too, picked myself up and went after after him. And where was Barry headed in such a hurry? I thought I knew the answer. Barry was off to mow the meadow, mow the meadow. And I followed as fast as I could.

Moaning Cave

The little house Cathy bought sat on a knoll or small bluff overlooking the town of Sonora Springs, deep in the Mother Lode country of the Sierra foothills. Near Cathy's house was Moaning Cave, a gaping limestone hole that wound three hundred feet into the hillside. In the old days one of its mouths farther up the bluff would give out long, eerie, not-quite-human sighs when the wind was blowing; that was how the cave got its name. The family who owned the property boarded up this opening and charged admission to the main entrance. In the late forties and fifties, when Sonora Springs had briefly meta-morphosed from Mother Lode ghost town to booming tourist spot, the owners had built an iron staircase all the way to the bottom of the main cave, where hundreds of Indian skeletons, so tradition claimed, once littered the floor.

Cathy paid her dollar fifty one morning, walked down the staircase after a family that had just driven up in their Winnebago, and dutifully examined spotlit stalactites — a sailboat, a baby carriage, Mussolini's nose. Then their guide, a teenage girl, shut off the lights so that they could experience a minute of darkness three hundred feet under the earth. Silence. Then she flipped the lights back on and they all trudged back up the staircase, shoes clanging on the metal steps.

On her afternoon walks through the dry foothill scrub and madrone trees, Cathy would pass the old boarded-up mouth on the knoll above the big cave. The boards looked like a gag, she thought. She longed to pry them off and let the cave cry out again.

But she did nothing of the sort. Instead, one lonely late spring evening soon after her move, she walked into the only bar in Sonora Springs. It was a strange place, with a pool table in the front room and lurid neon stalactites glowing aqua and violet over the bar — another relic, she supposed, from the town's fitfully prosperous past.

She sat down at the bar next to a man in a lumberjack shirt and jeans who was talking to a well-dressed couple on his right. They looked at Cathy as she slipped onto the stool, then continued their conversation.

Suddenly the man banged his fist on the bar counter, rattling the glasses. "Doesn't know a plumber's joint from his own joint, the turkey!"

Cathy turned to look at him.

"Sorry," he laughed.

He was big young man, heavyset, with a full black beard, piercing blue eyes, and teeth that looked perpetually clenched. Yet there was something very agreeable about him, too. Cathy thought of the blacksmith Vulcan, ruled by Mars.

The man on his right, middle-aged and moon

faced with a big potato nose, said, "Pay no attention."

Cathy smiled demurely. She had not minded.

"New here?" her neighbour asked briskly. There
was no trace of flirtation in his voice. As usual,
Cathy thought, her age had registered unfavourably.
Though her body was trim and youthful, she was
fifty-five and her face showed it.

"Just a month or so."

The man on his other side said, "I'm Barney. This
is my wife, Alicia." A dark, angular little woman
nodded at Cathy. "And this is Ben." He waved a
hand at the big man.

Ben ignored the introduction. "Why haven't we
seen you around before?" he demanded.

Cathy smiled again and shrugged. In fact, she
hadn't known if local custom here approved of
women, older women, alone in bars. "I'm living in
the ranch bungalow on the hill," she said finally.

Ben nodded. A fact like that, something solid
instead of vagueness, seemed to please him. "Behind
Ace Hardware," he said, and kept nodding.

Encouraged, she continued: "I'm a painter."

Identical smiles, polite but cynical, appeared on
the faces of all three listeners. Cathy understood
why. Sonora Springs was a famous refuge of would-
be artists, writers, photographers. The locals would
have a quiet contempt for them, of course — it
would be a defence against the greater worldliness
of the outsiders. But Ben did not seem like a local;
in spite of his talk about plumbing, he had a fine,
cultured voice.

"Where's your studio?" he asked. She saw that he

was playing with her, hoping to trap her, expose her as one of the pretenders.

Cathy looked down. "I work at home." It would be a mistake, she sensed, to let drop the fact that she was established and even lived off her sales. Ben had made up his mind that she was a dilettante, and this idea seemed to please him.

When she looked up a moment later, a small hand with lacquered pink nails lay on Ben's shoulder like a pet animal. A very young girl stood behind him. She wore jeans and a sleeveless top, and her fine brown hair hung to her waist. "So this is where you've been hiding," she laughed gaily. The pain in her voice made Cathy turn away.

Hunched over his beer, Ben did not reply. The girl stood behind him for what seemed to Cathy a very long time. Then she was gone.

"Roll you for the next round," Ben said to Barney. He brought the dice cup down on the counter so hard that part of Cathy's gin and tonic spilled out of her glass. This time Ben did not apologise. He lost the game. "Put theirs on my tab," he called to the bartender, and was out the door without saying goodbye.

Alicia leaned over Barney. "What's your name, dear?" she said to Cathy. "We're art dealers."

Cathy moved over to Ben's stool, hot as a stove, and told them.

"Oh, my, why didn't you say so? Barney and I moved out here from Sausalito last year. You've seen our place, the old feed store. We do it just to keep our hands in. Aren't you from the Bay Area, too? Why'd you come up here?"

"I was driving though last year and liked it. I couldn't afford a decent place in the city."

"Your work's too good for the tourists we get here," Barney rumbled.

Cathy blushed. Her art had not been recognised until after the upheaval that followed her last child's departure from home and her divorce from her second husband. Like a child, she was still excited by success but did not know how to assert it properly to the world. She hoped Barney and Alicia would spread the word in Sonora Springs.

"Just wait till you meet our local characters," said Alicia.

"What about Ben? What does he do?"

Husband and wife exchanged a glance. Alicia said, "He came out here from New Jersey. He used to be some kind of engineer."

"Designed and built his own house out near Coffee Creek," said Barney. "Damn fine job, but it should have been finished two years ago. He could get a great job down in the Bay Area any time he wanted to."

Cathy understood, or thought she did. Both of her sons had dropped out of college to live the simple life. But they were very young, still in their twenties, and it was not so important for them yet.

Alicia said, with a little smirk: "Ben's divorced. He's our local heartbreaker."

"I guess this is like the kind of place you might come to if you'd just gotten divorced."

"It's boring up here," Barney pronounced. "People don't have enough to do. They start in on sex at eight and stop at eighty. Three hitches per capita is the average. It's only fifty miles to Reno."

His wife cleared her throat to say something. She had, Cathy felt, been mentally reviewing possible candidates. After a pause Alicia said, "There just aren't many unattached here in the over-forty set, unfortunately."

Cathy did not feel this was the time to reveal her penchant for younger — much younger — men. It caused no comment in San Francisco, but she knew very well what it would do in a small town like this. She sighed inwardly and resigned herself in advance to becoming notorious, like Ben.

"There's a wonderful attorney friend of ours, retired, over in Angel's Camp. His wife died last year — "

Politely, Cathy listened.

Alone in her house, deeply involved in her work, Cathy painted every day. It was shaping up into an ascetic summer. Never before had she gone so long without the company of a man, and she found her mind wandering back to those who had played such a big part in her past. Cathy had always been indulgent, had always given in to men — either by nature or upbringing, it was too ingrained now to say which. Both her husbands had been very successful and she, feeling delight and self-hatred, had reflected off them like the moon. The sun and the moon. And the final freeing of her art had been less an act of will than simply what was left after the losses — of youthful beauty, children to care for, the husbands themselves. Life had conspired to take them away from her, so that she could get on with it.

She knew that. But the regret ran very deep.

The second husband, the Jewish one, had been a little warmer and more sentimental than the first. He had always encouraged her to get on with her "career," bought her paints for her birthday (the wrong kind), paid for classes at the Art Institute, got his friends to buy her paintings at very decent prices. She had produced even less during that marriage than she had during her first, with the husband who didn't give a damn about art and wasn't afraid to say so.

Ben, she reflected during breaks, was an interesting case. Here was a man cast in the same achiever mold as her husbands doing odd jobs in a tiny California foothill town. But the low-key life had not seemed to soften his personality; you felt he would tackle a clogged toilet with the same merciless energy as the second husband applied to People of California *v.* whatever. What was he doing here?

Cathy dropped into the bar almost every night now. The girl with the long brown hair no longer came to stand silently behind Ben. His latest seemed to be a woman in her thirties with a face of slightly haggard sensitivity. Cathy had seen this woman around town; she wrote children's books and wore her long blonde hair with ribbons in it. The writer never came to the bar — that showed a certain restraint, Cathy thought — but she and Ben had been seen together in the local breakfast spot sharing morning coffee and stilted conversation.

But that connection lasted only a few weeks. Soon Ben was back with his girls. Cathy observed him closely at the bar. Something kept appearing in the back of her mind when she saw him focus his predatory attention on a new fawn, something the reverse of the actual scene. What was it? The secret kept slipping away.

"You're watching me," he accused her one evening.

"Yes," she admitted.

"What do you see?"

Cathy smiled and looked down at her drink. She could never think of those quick replies, she was easily dominated in conversation. Friends said it kept her youthful. She knew it was something else, a kind of primitive function she had no control over.

"You're so quiet, you must see a lot," said Ben. "Tell me what you see."

At first Cathy did not answer. Now that he knew who she was, he liked to show her what he knew about art. When he was done giving his opinion, he would listen to her in turn, but the deference was slightly resentful. Cathy sensed Ben's disappointment. He had preferred her, as a woman, to be a delightful dabbler, not a disciplined artist, and that hooked all too easily into her old patterns.

"Why do you want to know what I see?" she asked finally.

"You're a very observant woman. I want to know what's going through your mind when you sit there like that."

"Well, I — "

Cathy stopped. Her mind had gone blank. A few moments passed while Ben watched her, unsmiling. Finally she seized a topic. "Have you ever been to Moaning Cave?"

"Moaning Cave!" he bellowed. "What a blight on

the face on the earth. I'd like to plant five sticks of high-grade dynamite at the bottom and blow it sky high!"

His unexpected violence startled Cathy. She rather liked Moaning Cave and still wanted to hear what the old abandoned mouth sounded like when the wind blew through it. "Why would you want to do a thing like that?"

"It ruins the structural integrity of the hill, that's why."

Cathy did not understand this, but she said nothing.

"It's a pesthole," he went on. "There's no point sinking for wells, it causes erosion. Rats breed in the upper chambers. It's ugly and it's useless. What I'd really like to do is bulldoze the whole thing in with fill."

"That's not very ecological," Cathy teased. Like every other outsider in Sonora Springs, Ben was an ardent conservationist.

He gave an irritated little shrug. "What about this little hole you're sitting in right now?" she ventured boldly.

Ben emitted the kind of noise you make when you drop a hammer on your thumb. "This place ought to be dynamited, too." He motioned at the neon stalactites. "I wish I didn't come here so often. Enclosed places give me the creeps. I have — what's the word?" Casually, he laid his hand on Cathy's arm; he was being charming again. Cathy knew the word but saw he wanted to be the one to say it. "Claustrophobia."

He smiled. Cathy watched his jutting teeth flash

in the dim little room. Oddly, it did not seem menacing. She wanted to say: You don't have to be afraid with me.

And before you knew it, summer was over. The grass in the pastures turned yellow, the air grew stinging cold. Most of the trees in this foothill country were pines and live oaks that stayed dusty green, but here and there on the hillside by Cathy's house she could spot a lone maple or birch blazing away in solitary splendour — a bit, she felt, like the transplanted Easterners in town.

One September afternoon Cathy and Alicia — two old women in jeans and down jackets, she thought self-consciously — walked slowly through Cathy's favourite cow pasture at the top of the hill, where the land was almost flat. The field was strewn with junk from the town's heyday — carriage wheels, pump parts, bedsprings. Sadness oozed from these rusty old pieces of iron lying out exposed to the air, soon to be covered by another season's snow. How had they lasted so long?

"Well, just look at Mr. Rabbit over there!" Alicia cried with false cheeriness. Cathy looked at the scrub near the fence where her friend pointed but saw nothing. It didn't seem to matter, though, because Alicia had just burst into noisy tears.

Cathy had suspected some sort of self-revelation was in the works since this morning at the post office, when Alicia had humbly asked for permission to accompany Cathy on her afternoon walk.

"Why, what's the matter?" Cathy said, putting her arm around the other woman's shoulders. People were sharp at seeing that she was good in this role and then engineering her into it.

"Oh, Cathy, I've just had the most awful relationship!"

For a second Cathy thought she meant Barney. But of course one did not talk that way of a thirty-year union.

"How terrible. Did you just break it off?"

Alicia was choking on her tears. She took a deep breath of air and then gagged, as if poisoned. "*He* broke it off," she moaned.

Cathy sighed. How many times had she seen other women, herself, in this state? What did it mean, all this love misery? Was it supposed to show you that you were bad and weak? Or good and strong? Both possibilities seemed equally likely.

On cue, she said: "Do you want to talk about it?"

Alicia shook her head vigorously, but this, Cathy knew, was just preliminary coyness. She resigned herself to an afternoon of missed painting.

The two women had stopped in the middle of the field at a huge scarred granite boulder deposited a few million years ago by some forgotten glacier. They sat down side by side on the great rock. The coldness of ancient stone crept through the seat of Cathy's jeans to her tender skin.

Alicia blew her nose and muttered under her breath. Cathy could not make out all the words. First came: "What a bastard, what a bastard," over and over again, then: "First he wouldn't — she was right *there* — nothing, not one thing!"

Cathy settled down to listen. A whole flock of hawks or turkey vultures, she could never tell which, made great lazy circles over the field. Cathy had learned that the big birds were not necessarily hunting something down below when they did that; they were merely amusing themselves with the thermals. Playing. She had never seen a place with so many of them as here in the Mother Lode.

The man in question, it turned out, had begun a passionate affair with Alicia a month before — the greatest high of her life — and just now, with no explanations, had cut her off as quickly as he had taken her up. And had started in with someone else. It was like day and night, Alicia said. Like going from a sauna to a deep freeze. Like jumping out of a plane in a parachute and hitting ground ten feet below. Nothing, she said, nothing could explain passion followed by such complete withdrawal.

"Who is he?" said Cathy, though she had a dreadful suspicion.

Alicia took a deep breath and looked away. "Who else?"

"How could you, Alicia!" Cathy could not stop herself. "You told me what he was like, you warned *me*."

Alicia could not meet her eye. "You always think you're the one who's going to be different with a guy like that," she laughed, bitterly.

Cathy was shocked. In a small way, she felt jealous. Watching Ben over the summer, she realised, she had come to feel the slightest bit possessive of him. His young girls were all very well, but *she* was the one who challenged and understood him. And all while they had been having their earnest chats in the bar, he had been carrying on with Alicia.

Alicia had been talking for some time. Guiltily, Cathy tuned back in. "Then he brought that waitress from Copperopolis home and there they were when I came to the door — "

"He must have really wanted to hurt you," Cathy said. Ordinary as it was, she was always struck by this kind of behaviour. Being mean took energy. People usually didn't bother unless they were trying to prove something.

Alicia was in no mood to appreciate the finer points. "Cathy, I've got to leave, get out of town. I can't face him every day in the post office, the bar — it's killing me! What am I going to do?"

"Why don't you go on an art-buying trip down to Los Angeles or somewhere?" said Cathy. "Go for a couple of weeks. Maybe it won't seem so bad when you get back."

"I always felt like he resented me or something. But I was so good to him. I don't see why he felt that way — why he treated me like that — "

A new tide of grief seemed to be rising, so Cathy said: "Now I remember. You were helping him buy some paintings for his living room."

"A watercolour and a nice little etching," said Alicia, distracted for the moment. "Lots of consulting. You know. He kept talking about buying a couple of your paintings, Cathy. He talked about you a lot. Asked me questions about who you were seeing. You know how he plays women off against each other. He tried to make me feel bad because I was the gallery person and you were the painter."

Cathy, who had always felt stupid and unsophisticated around Alicia, was surprised to learn of this unsuspected advantage. She tried hard to suppress a little glow of excitement in the pit of her stomach.

The rock had made her legs numb. Cathy jumped off it and started pacing up and down, restless. Reluctantly, Alicia struggled to her feet and they started back down the hill together. "You're right, of course," Alicia said wearily as they picked their way through the dried cow turds and bleached hummocks of grass. "What I need is to go to L.A. And get an eyelift."

Cathy had parked her car on the shoulder off the main road. She did not trust her old Datsun's suspension on the pitted dirt driveway that wound along Coffee Creek to the house that rose, all windows and hard angles, at the end. She walked down the driveway listening to the water gurgling through the rocks. Something dreary about that sharp little noise in the middle of the silent wilderness made her think of childhood, defeat. She carried a painting in each hand wrapped in newspaper and masking tape.

The house was made of redwood so weathered it looked like it had been beaten with chains. The front door was impossible to find. Was it this recessed alcove, or that sliding door? Ben was nowhere in sight. She knocked on random surfaces. The wood was so thick and solid it muffled the little sound completely. Cathy got splinters in her knuckles. Then she heard hammering. She picked her way around piles of lumber to the back of the house.

Ben was on his knees inside a ring of sawhorses and power tools, nailing a fresh piece of wood into a brand new deck. He did not look up from his task even though she knew he had heard her coming, a fact that amused Cathy.

"I've brought the paintings."

Now the bright blue eyes met hers. "Let's go in and have a beer," he said. Tamely, Cathy followed Ben into the house. Inside it was one enormous three-story room with a slate rock fireplace. Directly in front of the fireplace stood a great oak platform. His bed. It looked, Cathy thought, like an altar. Dog-eared science fiction paperbacks, empty beer cans, full ashtrays cluttered the floor. The room was cold, dank. Even with the bed it reminded Cathy of a warehouse.

Ben handed her an icy Coors and they sat down together on a broad windowseat. Except for the bed and a cracked black vinyl beanbag chair, the room had no furniture.

"Well, this is quite a place."

Ben gave a bluff laugh. "Someday I'll get organised." He was proud of its bleakness, she saw. He took the paintings from her and slit the newspaper wrappings delicately with a Swiss Army knife.

"Here I've paid all this money and haven't even seen what they look like," he joked, balling up the newspapers and tossing them carelessly in the corner. Ben had commissioned her to do two renderings of scenes around Sonora Springs — nature, *not* people — but otherwise the subject matter was to be at her discretion. That had been nice of him; most people were distressingly specific.

He stood the two unwrapped paintings up against the posts — pilings, actually — that held up the bed and backed off to inspect them. Cathy's style was one of technically exacting superrealism (people were always telling her how unlike her pliant personality her art was), and it was easy enough to place the first one, fussy pine tree needles pricking a cobalt heaven. Ben looked at it and nodded. But the other puzzled and upset him, she could see: the vortex that looks soft and inviting but is cold as death at the bottom. "What's that supposed to be?" Cathy smiled and shook her head. "I don't title them."

"It's going to haunt me till I figure it out." Ben walked over and stood deliberately close. "What if I make you tell me?"

Cathy looked up at him and a strange thing happened. In less than a second all sorts of information got passed back and forth. Ben's look said one thing, Cathy's said something else. Cathy saw him clench those splayed teeth — thumbsucker, she thought in secret contempt — and the hatred that rose out of him was so intense it would have withered her had she not clearly seen the fear and helplessness beneath it. For she was the mother and she owned him.

She let Ben put his hands around her waist and pull her slowly to her feet. In her years Cathy had had plenty of time to observe mothers and sons, particularly since she — and, when she thought about it, almost every other woman she knew — seemed to have been so much more successful as a mother than as a wife. Alicia, Cathy remembered, had a grown son, too. But Alicia had not read the fine print in this transaction.

Later, when they were lying side by side in the big cold bed, Ben said: "What are you thinking?" He was not really interested; she could tell by the sound of his voice he thought he had won again. Cathy smiled to herself and said nothing. She let the full effect of her silence envelop him. The darkness that had swallowed him up.

Halloween Notes

Sunday, October 30, 4 p.m. Anticipating costume ambivalence (something to wear or maybe not wear, but keep in my pocket just in case?), purchase glitter eye mask at Long's, $2.49 plus tax.

Monday, October 31, dusk (6:30 p.m.? Check tide tables.) Pull into Waldo Point Harbour parking lot, Sausalito. Party tonight courtesy the Bay Beasties, a group of older Marin County women who meet for a monthly ride in Richardson Bay on Mary Malone's tugboat tender *Baulinas*.

Memory flash of last meeting: Feet lodged in scuppers, leaning too far over the side watching the black water race by. Scuppers need work. State of mind: Drunken stupor. Alcatraz, badly lit, looming ahead like some medieval ruin — what was that island off the French coast, you walk out to it at low tide? Dark Angel Island to the left, port or whatever, blotting out East Bay hills behind it, fun.

Already this evening the Waldo Point parking lot is full of acronyms (SUVs, BMWs, etc.), so turn off into the unpaved, deeply rutted Gate 5 parking lot. Plenty of room here among the old Dodge Darts,

Camaros, Ford pickups. In days of yore the "hitch-hookers" operated out of this lot, thumbing rides at the freeway entrance in their boots and hot pants and bright makeup until finally it was too outrageous even for this town and the police shooed them away. Park, lock. Trip over something that squawks. Black rooster with red wattles scuttles into the weeds. Dirt trail wends off in the darkness toward the unlit maze of half-sunken docks and decrepit walkways over algae-clogged water connecting the darkened hulks — well, *funky* scarcely begins to describe an area that looks like the aftermath of an H-bomb hit. Gate 5, still hanging in after all these years. Only big change: they finally tore down the hulk of a steamboat that plied the American and Sacramento rivers in the 1920s and ended up beached here like a sepulchral estate marker. What's left? The old paddlewheel, repainted brick red with the name emblazoned on its upended side: *Charles Van Damme.*

Buzz into the locked entrance of the Yellow Ferry dock — a.k.a. Gate 6, from the World War II days when these docks were all part of the Marinway shipyards — follow the main dock lined with architect-designed houseboats, all light and airy with their skylights, seventies stained glass, bubble solariums. Not many pumpkins, but I encounter an early patrol of unsupervised humans: skeleton, ballerina, alien. None over four feet high. Where is the parent? What if they fall in the water?

6:09 p.m. Arrive at Babs's houseboat, about halfway out the dock. Weathered wood shingles, big windows, some sort of flying buttress around the side, expensive. Knock on the open front door, walk down a corridor hung with textiles from someplace or other to the two-story galley/living room. Spectacular view of harbour, bay, the San Francisco skyline. Babs fixing a plate of raw vegetables that resonates perfectly in colour and texture with the living room's ethnic art and masks and Japanese pillows. Each carrot and celery stick Cuisinart-cut and laid in piles of excruciatingly precise proportions. Lettuce beautifully streaked with white, looks batiked. Does Babs have a matching shirt in her closet? All Sausalito women with any money make hors d'ouevres like this and have houses, floating or on the ground, like this — totally controlled aesthetic environments, not a hair or radish out of place. No men in sight. Note to self: coincidence?

Babs to me: "Did I tell you? The kayak clubs are trick-or-treating. They paddle through the whole marina."

Self to Babs: "Where's Ruth?" This meant as gentle joke in reference to the oldest member of the Bay Beasties, usually first at the parties.

A look crosses Babs's face. "Ruth is dead."

Expression on my face a call for further explanation. "Her daughter found the body this morning in her condo. Heart attack." Babs hands me a glass of Cakebread Sauvignon Blanc. "Ruth wouldn't have wanted us to cancel just because of her. You know how she loved these parties."

Ghost face, crimson lips. Moment of panic, then clarity. Note to self: Remember the clown seminar.

Light touch on my shoulder. "Look, look!"

Out of the darkness on the other side of the living room window appears a vision: a moving deck complete with chair, geranium planter, and man operating an outboard motor. It's Babs's neighbour Jack, the real estate agent. Last summer Jack discovered (1) that his deck floated, and (2) that he could detach the deck from his houseboat. Has cruised the marina nightly ever since.

Brown bottle of Fat Weasel Ale in one hand, Jack ties off at the piling with the other. Hops onto Babs's nondetachable deck, walks into the living room, plops himself down on the white duck divan in his cords, turtleneck and down Patagonia vest. Babs looks at him severely. A dramatic ratted Rastifarian wig covers Jack's buzz cut. "What's that supposed to be?"

Jack looks proud. "I'm an Anchor Out!"

Anchor Outs — indigents whose scows, plastic-walled skiffs, and shanties on platforms float rent free some yards out from the end of Gate 5, its Ultima Thule. Every year or so the city of Sausalito requires indigent owners to prove these sorry structures are mobile and thus legally "boats" by motoring, rowing, or towing them around a harbour buoy about 200 yards offshore. Event predictably produces a rich harvest of casualties — edifices that either refuse to move or, in moving, sink. Fleeting sense of pity. Who else in this country has to put his or her domicile through such a demanding test?

7:38 p.m. Now a dozen Bay Beasties mingle on the deck with Jack. Begins to feel like a party.

Cluster of lights way out in the bay has been moving closer and closer. A shout carries across the water. Around the end of Babs's dock, lights turn into twenty kayaks cutting through the cobweb of reflections in the still harbour water. The kayakers skirt Jack's deck piggybacked to the end of Babs's deck, pull up to the side instead. Their shells decorated Road Warrior style with homemade tribal totems, tinsel, pumpkin heads.

An awkward business passing over the treats, but Bay Beasties are nothing if not hostesses. Kayakers gulp down white wine (a few primly request mineral water), devour the smoked salmon. Vegetables and dip too complex to serve to people in moving vessels. Plus kayakers, mostly men, don't want them much.

Scarcely have the fellows left than another fleet of paddlers straggles into the harbour, up to the side of Babs's deck. Overall impression: tentlike ethnic matriarchal costumes worn over wetsuits and down vests. Do I spy a mask or two from the last Bolinas New Year's Mime? It's Mariah, the all-female kayaker club. Horned Isis asks to use the bathroom, clambers out of her shell with a self-conscious laugh and troops past us, wetsuit leaving a trail of icy water on Babs's white rug.

Now a jolly shout from inside. A white-haired man with a youthful face, jovial as Father Christmas, stands in the living room brandishing a bottle. He wears a maroon suit coat covered with campaign buttons. Babs cries, "Henry's here!"

We all feel happy to see Henry.

"Go around to Henry's," Babs orders the kayakers. "Henry will give you balloons!"

"Helium balloons!" cries Henry. He vanishes down the hall.

8:15 p.m. The kayakers push off. Nora and I leave Babs's to follow around on the dock to Henry's. Nora a Marin matriarch, divorced from professional husband but of the generation with no career of their own. Defining trait of Marin matriarch: Enormous house on a wooded hillside in the basement of which emotionally stunted adult children of either sex vegetate like mushrooms. With property tax virtually impossible to pay, there is frequent recourse to gallant, desperate measures. (Note to self: Remember the velvet-cloaked Marin matriarch who used to sweep into the franchise restaurant at the bottom of the hill in Mill Valley every Friday at dusk bearing a tray of her famous cheesecake. But even then fifty-two splendid cheesecakes did not equal the property tax, no they did not.) In Nora's case property tax is no longer a problem because the enormous house burned down, unfortunate consequence of one rash act in a lifetime of prudence: inviting home for the night that charming fellow from Smiley's bar out in Bolinas. He was well dressed, but an important question was not asked: What was he — what was she — doing in Smiley's? And though he was not actually robbing her, why did he torch the den curtains?

Henry's houseboat a formidable three-story edifice, rustic floating hunting lodge after the manner of William Randolph Hearst's country estate Wyntoon. No lights visible. Carved oak door swallows my feeble knocks. After many minutes, a wizened little fellow in a sleeveless jersey appears. Moment of nonrecognition. Then: Henry. Health and bonhomie gone with the party coat. Henry does not look happy about anything, least of all visitors. Lets us in nonetheless. Mixed message, this.

We walk silently through a cavernous living room, all dark timber paneling, massive fireplace stretching the length of the far wall. First impression: Is this a museum? Glass cases with tiers of miniature classic cars line the walls, ten-foot wooden statue of a woman on roller skates hovers above us. An ancient jukebox — no, four of them in a row, all in pristine condition, shiny household gods. Many other collections, all very still, all very dead. Not a hair out of place. Male version of Babs's houseboat.

Henry steers us out the other end of the living room onto a deck. Orange balloons fastened to the railing in tidy unjoyous symmetry. Nora asks: "Balloons for the kayakers?"

Henry clears his throat. "They're for decoration, actually. But sure, you can give them to the kayakers."

Who are just now pulling up alongside. Split personality manifestation as Henry abruptly switches into party mode: "Balloons, balloons!" We untie the balloons from the railing — with difficulty, he made the knots very tight — hand them out to the women of Mariah, who tie them on the prows and sterns. With Henry they don't linger. But they make a pretty sight, paddling off; bobbing orange globes last visible objects before night and the water swallow them up.

Silence falls. Nora and I say goodbye to Henry, walk alone through the mausoleum of a living room out onto the dock.

8:39 p.m. Back at Babs's, Jack is cranking up the outboard motor on his portable deck. Babs to Nora and me: "Why did you come back? We're just on our way over." Don't have the heart to report not much going on at Henry's. By this time a neighbour has shown up with children, real children — the skeleton, ballerina, and alien. They march out onto Babs's deck and climb over onto Jack's deck, followed by the only two Bay Beasties in costume: French maid and real German woman in a retro black and white cocktail dress and spike heels. All showing off for Jack, the only man. German woman makes especially pretty jump from Babs's deck onto his deck.

Our skipper backs up his deck into the harbour, points it bayward. As we head briskly past the quiet line of houseboats, the children stand up in the middle of the barge, strangely blasé about this adventure. Question: Will any of the kids in class the next day believe them? Maybe Sausalito kids are pretty much burned out on this sort of thing, all of them having whimsical rich bohemian-emulating parents, etc.

In the middle of the bay the dark outline of faux palm trees on a rounded bulk: Kidd's Island. The ultimate Anchor Out, a rich man's Captain Nemo fantasy. Rubberised island on top, three-story underwater mansion below, grand pianos, viewing windows at every level, the works. Always my ambition to be invited to one of Kidd's famous parties; never quite happened. Note to self: Upgrade social life?

9:21 p.m. From Babs's to Henry's at the end of the dock is a disappointingly short trip. Question: Why did I come back? Answer not immediately forthcoming. Henry stands where we left him out on his deck. Expression on seeing a deckful of partygoers arrive: enigmatic. Children file into the living room; skeleton and alien peel off toward the classic cars. Henry takes rest of us for a guided tour of the whole place. Has owned it less than a year, he tells us. Jack was his agent. "The deal I got him!" Jack whispers.

Top floor all tatami mats and sliding doors. Over a low enormous bed an orange Japanese wedding dress hangs like an empty shroud. Bathroom given over to a magnificent *furo* in green tile.

Down pretty little winding stairs, varnished as all wood must be on the water, to the lowest of the three floors. Two more perfect bedrooms here, one black leather and one French country. The black leather bedroom has a bathroom with an elegant wallpaper pattern of — visible only on closer inspection — fornicating samurai. I block the ballerina from entering, make her mother take her to the toilet upstairs. Then close the door to have a pee myself. The porthole offers a cameo of the broker's enormous white houseboat at the next dock. Broker keeps a speedboat on the lower deck and a landing pad for his helicopter on the upper deck. Next to him, a two-story houseboat whose lower level, all lit up, is a single long room that is nothing but an enormous closet. In the closet, one end to the other, nothing but men's suits. A young man dressed in tennis whites skips down the stairs, two more suits thrown over his arm.

Turn away from East Egg vision, close the bath-room door firmly behind me.

Jack standing in the hallway — waiting for the john? But he doesn't move. Takes a swallow from a new Fat Weasel. "Wesley Oyama built this place," he tells me. Delivers a quiet belch. "Isn't it something?"

"So why did he sell?" Always the troubling thing about these luxury properties — people pour in/out their souls/money, then turn around and sell.

"Well," Jack says, "Wesley died. His heirs wanted to unload." He shakes his head; it almost seems too much for him. "The deal I got Henry."

Back on the main floor, light rims a doorway at the other side of the big gloomy living room. Peek in. A tiny, messy bachelor galley strewn with papers and trash, deli containers of half-eaten pasta salad, paperback thrillers embossed with shiny metallic lettering lying open spine up on the floor. Revelation: This is where Henry actually lives, the only safe place on board. This is an AIDS houseboat, Jack cut Henry an AIDS deal. Rest of floating mansion unsafe, ruled by shadows.

The children look bored. Like their motorised deck ride, this dark Disneyland does not awe them as much as might be expected. No fake spider webs hanging from the rafters, no Jack-o-Lanterns, no candy, no nothing except the now-decimated row of balloons outside. All file out to the movable deck. Jack invites Henry to ride with us back over to Babs's.

"No, thanks," Henry says. "I think I feel like staying here by myself."

Waves goodbye from his deck, a tiny figure.

On the way back I spot another full bottle of Fat Weasel poking out of the mossy lining of a ficus planter. Pick it up playfully, suggest christening the deck. First real emotion I have seen appears on Jack's face: "You're going to give that more bubbles than champagne!" Put bottle back in the planter.

11:05 p.m. We tie up at Babs's, disembark. The children, sleepy, are taken down the dock to their own houseboat. Once they are gone, all present seized by the need to convince ourselves that this was the most special night of the children's lives. Babs, eagerly: "I heard Tara say, *This is the best Halloween I ever had!*" Laughter, nods. Babs repeats, "'The best Halloween I *ever* had'!"

Mary and Babs raise their glasses to Ruth, a gallant lady. Mary looks up at the misted skylight: "Wherever you are." She herself has decided only this week to divorce her husband, who has not given up touring the Marianas on his 50-foot wooden schooner as he promised Mary he would. Ruth had been a sailing widow, too. Her husband, now a widower himself though he does not know it yet, is tacking somewhere off Eleuthera in the company of his young mistress.

One of the few remaining Bay Beasties proposes going to Horizons to look at the Halloween costumes. She and the German woman in the tight dress are engaged in knee-jerk flirting activities with Jack. Babs's sharp ears pick up this exchange. "Go on!" she says to Jack in a kidding tone. "Take your two little popsies to Horizons!" (Tone in fact friendlier than it looks written down in black and white like this.)

11:50 p.m. Next-to-last exchange of the evening, Jack to me: "Six-fifty. That's what Henry got it for. After Wesley put a mil plus into it."

11:52 p.m. I walk down the empty dock into the brightly lit Waldo Harbour parking lot. Reach for car keys, touch rough surface of totally forgotten glitter mask in jacket pocket. In Gate 5 parking lot on the other side of the bushes a shabby group of people are drinking. Their voices carry in the dark, but not their words.

Memory flash: The clown seminar. Ruth was in it, so were Babs and Nora and Mary. In the old days a self-described ex-circus performer out in Stinson Beach held two-week workshops on how to be a clown: making the costume, putting on the makeup, learning a routine or two, but most importantly discovering the spontaneity of *clownfulness*, losing identity in the holy ritual of clowning, fun. Heard the ladies were motoring out to Stinson twice a week to learn the craft, but forgot all about it until that day, rounding the corner from Highway 1. Hanging out the windows of Mary's stately old Beamer, a veritable gaggle of clowns. Whiteface and outsized painted lips and orange string wigs all startlingly bright in the foggy coastal air. But only faint cheers, tentative clownlike laughs, in striking contrast to vehicle's confident Germanic growl pulling into the post office parking lot. Foursome piles out in quest of an audience; their instructor, in mufti, remains prudently in the front passenger seat. Midday rush to the P.O. over, only a solitary carpenter standing next to mud-spattered pickup. Stands impassive, arms folded, as clowns rush and tumble past. Carpenter's studied lack of reaction freaks them. One clown even trips over his workboot, possibly not intentionally placed in the way. Babs (recognisable because trimmest and most agile) does fair cartwheel, clown pants sagging over her head almost to the ground. Cartwheel makes young black lab in back of pickup bark and keep on barking.

11:58 p.m. Back in the Gate Five parking lot, memory flash interrupted by a tall boy wearing jeans who carries his liquor in a paper bag with the top rolled down over the mouth of the bottle. "Jodi's thing still going down?" he asks. Then gets close enough to see I belong to a different gate. The Yellow Ferry gate. "Never mind." Walks back into darkness.

11:59 p.m. Almost to my car now, still gripped by the past: Clown group making a quick turn around the deserted Stinson Beach parking lot, embarrassed hellos to me in passing, then all piling back to safety in the Beamer. Dog in pickup still barking as car roars away. Framed in the receding rear window, one whiteface peers back at me, mouths silent words through huge smiling maroon lips, points a gloved finger at herself with grave emphasis, I don't understand — you, is that you, Ruth?

Flightless Birds

The moa sat in a glass case next to Phar Lap — Phar Lap's skeleton, that is; the bones of the famous racing stallion caught my eye first. Phar Lap had been a very big horse, to judge by those bones. His heart, a notice explained, was buried across the Tasman Sea in Melbourne; a third country was the resting place for other, unnamed organs. At first I took Phar Lap for a dinosaur and the moa for something that might still be with us. Just being stuffed made the moa seem more modern and plausible: a ten-foot bird with big legs and no wings, why not? It was a fairytale nightmare, but a gentle one. Tiny head, elongated neck, disproportionately heavy thighs, a benign reptile rising out of a pair of oversized feathered hipboots. The three-toed leathery claws at the end of those legs measured a good foot across. Dun-coloured feathers sprouted from a huge pouty breast. Where the wings should have been were only more feathers.

I felt, just then, a jolt, a spurt of anxiety so primal it made me think the ground of this highly seismic little country was quivering beneath the museum's marble floor.

> Bonnie laddie, will ye go?
> Will ye go, will ye go?
> To the birks of Aberfeldie?

An image rose from nowhere. A blonde Scotsman in a white suit, pedalling his bicycle down a suburban street. In its glass cage the moa cast a giant's shadow on half a hill of faux countryside. Its large, expressive eye was impossible to meet.

Riding north from Wellington on the big Road Services bus the next day, I tried to picture this enormous clumsy fowl loping across the real landscape — green, heaving, volcanic — that unrolled before me. The moa's forest habitat had been gone two hundred years, of course. There was only pastureland now, a wide net of dairy and sheep farms spread out in the shadow of the cloud-shrouded mountain called Taranaki. Every time I looked at Taranaki, it seemed to be sending me messages, important messages, in code. Not the kind a madman gets but something deeper, some important information about the natural world. I looked hard. Moment by moment a cloud mass wrapped and unwrapped itself around the bulk of the great mountain, popping one picture after another into the cheap iron window frame. Foreground, a flock of blinding white goats in a green field. Background, Cloud & Mountain, 725 variations. And this meant something. But what?

Cyclone Bola, first storm of the autumn season — it was the second week of March — stranded me in New Plymouth. For three days heavy rain fell, scattered in all directions by a gusty, severe, unpredictable wind. When the roads were open again I pushed on to Sheperton, an inland agricultural and college town I had visited on a similar junket six years before, end point of my government-sponsored tour of school districts on the North Island.

The bright red bus flashed through a gleaming countryside of heavily grazed hills and steep-terraced little gulches choked with tree ferns. The wet ground stank everywhere of sheep. We passed a lone warehouse bearing an ancient stencilled sign, "Elder's Pastoral Woolbrokers," on its corrugated iron roof, crossed a high-running river, and pulled into the coastal town of Wanganui. I bought a copy of the previous day's newspaper at the Station Hotel's Flagon Bar and Bottle Store. The front page was full of stories about the flooding around the country. Families in outlying regions had been stranded for days without electricity. Black Power, the Maori motorcycle gang, had helped with the cleanup in Gisborne. A smudgy photo caught my eye: a blanketed human shape, lying on the Manawatu bank.

Watercolour-green New Zealand lies directly in the path of the South Pacific prevailing winds. These nameless gusts of atmospheric spirit routinely blow huts and people off the mountains of the South Island. On the North Island they roar through the Manawatu Gulch, a deep earth crack whose winding river, bursting with rain during Cyclone Bola, had disgorged the body of Dougal McDougal on a soggy embankment.

The unusual repeating measure of the victim's name meant nothing at first. I thought idly how the

Highland Scots and the Maoris, many of whose descendants had intermarried here, uncannily resembled each other. A good Maori name like Tumoana Tumoana, why, it was absolutely the same thing, those fierce clans with their kilts, wool or feathered, and their honour and their land and all the rest of it. Mountain songs the world over sound alike, said a poet, because they describe the same spirits.

Not until the bus was rolling again in open country did the image rise up again, surface in my own Manawatu.

> Sweet are the banks, the banks o' Doon
> The spreading flowers are fair,
> And everything is blythe and glad,
> But I am fu' o' care.

Blonde hair, white suit, bicycle. And a pang born of connection, of recollection. Him, drowned? The thought of such a grotesque accident struck me deeply.

A lunch shared six years before offered no special reason to remember Dougal McDougal. Face? Gone. Truly gone now, the thought came. What lingered was a kind of aura, a certain anomaly of situation — a doctor of divinity from Edinburgh teaching in a provincial New Zealand high school. And the persistent image. Blonde hair, white suit, bicycle, a figure moving down a summer street.

That intense rainless wind, aftermath of the cyclone, bent the bushes flat as our bus pulled into the Sheperton station. During my previous visit, in a field not far from the centre of town, a woman had

been found dead of mysterious wounds. The homi-
cide investigation determined she had been gored by
a bull while taking an ill-advised shortcut to the
bank. Verdict, death by misadventure. Sitting with
my bag in the terminal waiting room, I had worked
up a whole theory about this country's random toll
of human sacrifice as my friend Graeme walked up.
Graeme's pencil-thin moustache gave him the rakish look of a lounge lizard. In reality he was a
shrivelled hazelnut of a professor with a mother up
the Wairapa. It was Graeme who had introduced me
to Dougal McDougal on my trip six years before.

Pecking me quickly on the cheek, Graeme was on
the subject right away. "Dougal didn't *jump* in the
river," he told me as he stowed my suitcase in the
boot of his right-hand drive Ford Escort. "He lay
down on the embankment and shot himself through
the mouth. The river rose up and washed him down-
stream." Just the day before Graeme had identified
the body, and he was still shaken by the experience.
We went to his house and sat in the living room as
the wind blew hard outside. An electric heater the
size of a jukebox issued a loud sterile hum; abun-
dant hydro resources made electricity very cheap in
New Zealand.

Graeme bustled in the kitchen fixing tea. Ten
years before, he had taught with my then-husband
at San Francisco State as an exchange professor. We
became friends and Graeme had fixed up my first
trip to New Zealand after my divorce.

Awkward, I thought, showing up for a visit smack
in the middle of a tragedy. But Graeme, it turned
out, had not been at all close to the deceased — had

scarcely seen him in previous months — though everyone else, including Dougal McDougal himself, who had left a note addressed to Graeme, now seemed to regard them as bosom buddies. Dougal McDougal was also unmarried, and there had been virtually no family to notify — an aunt in Inverness — but still. In Graeme's life it was not a tragedy but the echo of a tragedy. Dougal's tragedy was Graeme's misadventure. It would be Graeme's task to sort through the belongings, with sympathy but not with love.

Graeme went off to teach. After a bit I ventured out alone on the windswept streets of Sheperton, steering well clear of the Manawatu. It wasn't my tragedy either, but still. The funeral was scheduled in three days' time, which would be one day after my departure. The Maoris would have held a *tangi*, a wake. Go to one of those and you knew somebody was dead, for sure. No such luck for a Scottish bachelor, slipped into the ground, cremated, whatever, with genteel and subdued ceremony, no relatives engaged in keening or head banging or self-mutilation of the sort Polynesians once went in for. Though maybe more awaited him, after:

> When Death's dark stream I ferry o'er
> (A time that surely shall come)
> In Heaven itself I'll ask no more
> Than just a Highland welcome.

I had not yet asked Graeme "why" and he had volunteered no explanation except for a vague reference to the deceased's drinking habits. It seemed overcurious to wonder what was in the note when I had met the man only once. A lunch. I couldn't recall a thing either of us had said. And where did we eat that lunch? Somehow the Image, as I began to think of it, carried with it the information that he had been riding his bicycle away from the house I had stayed at in Sheperton, had been riding down my street. Had I made him a lunch? If it had been that personal, why didn't I remember it?

I passed a corner that held a "dairy" or convenience store. Next to it was a beauty salon bearing the name "Fantasy Unisex Hair Shoppe." Two workmen, one white, one Maori, were repairing the water main in the street. Both wore ragged old singlets, gumboots, shorts, and tights. Over the wind they shouted at each other in a wild dialect of this First World outpost I could not understand.

The wind. Mercurial, inconsistent blasts died to utter stillness, then rose again. This effect was more nervewracking, somehow, than a steady gale. So back I went to Graeme's empty house and turned on the toasting machine in the living room. To its pulsing rhythm I flipped through an odd collection of religious essays by the great New Zealand poet James K. Baxter. Spousal love within the dictates of the Church of England, that kind of thing. Creepy by virtue of the author's frantic but earnest attempts to cram himself into a dress suit that didn't fit. You didn't blame Baxter, finally, for saying the hell with it, turning into a hippie and founding a commune among the Maoris called New Jerusalem.

Dougal McDougal, D.D., would have been — was there such a thing as Church of Scotland? Well, of course there must be, maybe even a Kirk; we Yanks are so bad with these details. But unlike Baxter, Dougal McDougal had not rebelled by joining a commune. He seemed to have followed, initially, the earlier, time-honoured black sheep model: self-abasement via exile and obscurity in the colonies. He had "buried himself," as they say,

> Frae the friends and land I love
> Driv'n by Fortune's felly spite,

had thrown over everything to teach Latin to provincial teenagers way down here in the middle of a raw landscape and 80 million sheep. The familiarity of the pattern suggested scandal, flight — whatever that old dust-up might have been, now completely topped by this, the supreme scandal of his death.

In the late afternoon Graeme came back. Dark rainless clouds, the last scraps of *Cyclone Bola*, lowered on the other side of the window. The wind sank and lifted and sank again.

Besides the pills, said Graeme, Dougal had been dead drunk when he shot himself. I squirmed, on the slick Naugahyde of Graeme's easy chair, to contemplate the awful selfishness of suicides, who spare themselves but oppress strangers as well as intimates with the squalid details of their deaths.

> This worthless body damn'd himself
> To save the Lord the trouble.

"The note — " He stopped himself. I was glad. I no longer wanted to know what was in the note. Enough of Dougal.

In his note, Graeme went on, which was actually a kind of memorandum, Dougal had meticulously listed

100

the charities that were to receive his goods and effects. The car, a trusty Holden, was to be donated to Dougal's school's Pony Club. Graeme was now experiencing a frisson of doubt about whether the school would accept it. He would need, he added, to organise some help to go through the effects, sort and box them.

I cleared my throat. Surely that could wait until the weekend, until after the funeral, until I was safely gone? "I'll have to go over there tomorrow," Graeme said. "It's a little morbid, I know. Of course, if you don't want to — "

Well. I heaved a sigh. We ate a good dinner and I retired early to the guest room, where I

> dream'd I lay where flowers were springing
> Gaily in the sunny beam,
> List'ning to the wild birds singing,
> By a falling crystal stream.

Dougal McDougal looked straight into my eyes. He said my name: "Grace." That was all.

Next morning the wind was utterly gone. I looked out the window. Surely a New Eden stretched before my eyes. Branches pressed against the glass in pockets of shining water. The sun lit up the dewy green grass of Graeme's yard in a kind of luminous fury that spun me in a trance of supernal beauty.

The dazzle of the new-washed landscape had faded in my soul by the time we drove to Dougal's after breakfast. We pulled up in front of a small frame house. Weeds high enough to signal lack of attention but not eccentricity dotted the front yard. In the cement driveway sat a cream-coloured Holden soon to be spurned by a school club. The house itself was a nondescript bungalow, aggressively unpretentious like most dwellings in this country, intending stubbornly to signify neither upper nor lower.

We walked up the driveway. I might not remember Dougal McDougal's face, but I did retain an impression of his personality. Of — feyness? Was that the word? A Peter Pan quality. That ice cream suit. Charisma even. Back then Graeme had said — this much came back to me — Ring Dougal, you'll like him.

At a varnished front door Graeme took a set of keys from his pocket and fumbled with the lock. While he was performing a series of aborted manoeuvers the door sprang suddenly open and we walked into a bright white-walled living room. The interior of Dougal's house was familiar in a way its exterior was not. Here were books, tapes and compact discs, black-tube furniture, a table with a circle of glass on top instead of the ubiquitous 1950s New Zealand breakfast nook. Give or take a little sophistication, I could have been in Ann Arbor or Munich instead of looking out at the puekakis pecking desultorily at the seeds in Dougal's elegantly overgrown front yard.

As I took in the decor, something else began to impose itself — naggingly, like a horse fly — on my senses. I managed to ignore it the first five minutes or so as I watched Graeme haul out the cardboard boxes he'd stashed in the kitchen and set them up around the desk and bookshelves. An attractive paperweight on the desk caught Graeme's eye. As he stopped to heft it, the subliminal interference resumed.

It was a voice, a busy insistent voice muttering so fast that at first I had only the impression of a great rush of jabber, a muddy flood spilling through me. Where was it coming from? No red light lit up the stereo receiver; the dead television screen held only our distorted images and a small white explosion trying to copy the piece of sky that peeked through the window. The voice could not be coming from outside, either. High fences on both sides screened Dougal's house from the neighbours.

"...no fucking chance, he said, so I — yes *that's* right, naturally that's the way it was going, I could see it coming a mile off — so *I* said, 'If that's the way you feel about it you can go sod yourself! Sod yourself. And the whole lot with you.' And it was downhill from there, my dears, which is neither here nor there, the main point is *I* told *him* where to get off and he won't forget *that*, no, he..."

It was like being slapped in the face. I took an automatic step back into the foyer. The voice stopped abruptly. After a pause I leaned forward, experimentally, into the living room.

"Tasty little fuck..."

I stepped back quickly. Graeme, now bent over the kitchen sink, looked up. "Want to give us a hand in here?"

To get to the kitchen I had to cross the living room. The voice pursued me like an angry wasp. "Yes, I'm going to, going to, going to — "

"Could you just stack these dishes and things in the boxes there?"

Only a low murmur penetrated the tiny kitchen alcove, a rivulet that drowned out the sense of individual words. Though hardly reassuring, it made things, for the time being, bearable.

103

"Hear anything funny, Graeme? Humming or something?"

He cocked his head. "You mean the fridge?"

I had an idea. "Let's put on some music, shall we?"

The stereo was located in the dreaded living room, on a cluttered end table next to the slim black leather couch. I measured the distance from the kitchen. Putting my fingers in my ears would attract unwanted attention. "The Lord is my Shepherd," I said ridiculously. Then I plunged into the room, snapped on the radio, and darted out. Back in the kitchen the effect was satisfactory. A Schubert quintet on the national broadcast just managed to assert its authority over the residue of the hateful voice, which merged grudgingly with the bass line.

I settled down to a bit of silverware sorting, dish stacking. The voice said in my ear, shrilly and distinctly: "Eat shit!" The plate I dropped cracked in the sink.

Graeme looked up from an iron bucket full of empty vodka bottles. "Oh well, it was chipped anyway. Here, what's the matter?" For I had pushed past him out the kitchen door to sit down heavily on the steps. The back yard was a forest of overgrown lawn. Dark orange lemons, unpicked, hung rotting on a small tree. "Maybe I'm getting the flu," I muttered, trying to lay the groundwork for a speedy exit.

Obliging Graeme had a solution. "Why don't you have a liedown in the bedroom?"

The prospect of being assaulted by the voice while

104

in the prone position was too horrible to contemplate. "This house gives me the creeps."

"Does it really?"

"Yes, it does."

"Well." He considered reluctantly. "I suppose I don't have to do all of this today. Why don't I take you back home?"

I got to my feet at once and swept through the living room, now oddly still. Graeme, trailing in my wake, closed the windows and locked up. Once I was safely in his car, I wondered: Was this what they called an auditory hallucination? Or was it really possible I had heard Dougal? If so, then why? And why couldn't Graeme hear him? What had singled me out for this honour?

I remembered I had dreamed of Dougal, briefly, the night before. That is, I had heard him speak my name. His face hadn't been part of it. I had simply "known" it was Dougal. That word, my name, had been neutrally pronounced. It had carried no echo of this ugly gout of woe.

Another possibility had to be considered. The hateful voice could be something coming from inside me that I conveniently experienced as coming *to* me, from the outside. This, after all, is our modern view of such events. What lived in me, I dutifully asked myself, that would hook itself up to a suicidal Scotsman — to a shallow, vengeful, obsessive niggling and gnawing after this and that little detail of daily life?

Well, it is never hard to see these qualities in yourself, and I did. I *was* petty and obsessive, and on top of that I had been alone, too much alone.

Maybe that left room for a voice. These reflections brought me no relief. Nor did they cancel out the certainty that the voice still lay in wait over in Dougal's living room. If anything, that was proof it belonged to Dougal and not to me, for wouldn't I be hearing it everywhere if it were mine? — from, say, the amplifier-sized electric heater at Graeme's, a far more likely-looking instrument for transmitting messages from the Beyond?

Finally, if I were really hearing a spirit, why a garden-variety Western spirit, a pallid miserable little Protestant creature? Why not some sort of powerful Maori emanation in this land where many people listened very hard for the receding echoes of such voices? Was I doomed to receive only the petty whining cries of a soul from my own ethnic group — we who had made such a puny showing in this area for so many centuries?

I have no religion, I've never been baptised. Once after one of my education lectures at the adult evening school in Gardena an old man approached me. He and his wife had been arguing about which church they ought to go to, he said. He liked the Catholic church with the nice singing, but she preferred the Methodist congregation they had both been brought up in. After Jesus died, he asked me, brow furrowed, who was it that actually came first, the Catholics or the Protestants?

My grandparents were religious people. The pages of my grandmother's Bible were worn thin from constant turning. Once in a dentist's waiting room full of people she sank to her knees crying, "Everything is nothing!" and fainted, but my mother said that was because of what they'd given her for her root canal work. She's gone now. So's her religion. Churches look like banks these days. I told the old man, "I don't think it matters, do you?" But what if it did?

Graeme and I ate a meager dinner in a Chinese restaurant where the waiters wore dinner jackets, the chop suey was watery, and the tea was weak. The following morning I was due at the university to give my talk, "Education in the New Millennium?" — an engagement that would let me off the hook for any more Dougal-related activities. And that afternoon, weather permitting, I'd be gone, gone, gone.

I could not resist looking over at the heater when we walked in Graeme's door. But all that came out of it, when he flipped it on, was a comforting drone, God's vibrations as channelled by the torrents, falls, and streams of *belle* New Zealand.

"What sort of person was he, really?"

My friend's small face contorted slightly, causing his moustache to wiggle. "Dougal was — " he cleared his throat, "a good fellow."

"What do you mean by good?"

"Heavens, what do you think I mean? He was *good*. Helped people out. Lots of volunteer services. Save the environment, that was his thing. The disintegrating ozone layer. He had this bloody chart that showed how by the year 2030 there'd be absolutely no protective shield between us naked humans and the void. Bit of an alcohol problem — did I tell you that? And he got depressed — Lord, did he ever. I reckon that's when he must have done it, during one of his moods. He told me once he shut himself up in the closet when he got like that. Came out after a couple of days when it was over. Mainly he was just a nice chap. Didn't let you very close, but then who does?"

So Dougal was good, eh? Here was food for thought. Was that sad little voice in Dougal's living room the inevitable dark side, I wondered, his denied shadow self? Had I been turned into a convenient receptacle for the toxic waste, so to speak, of Dougal's goodness?

"Why did he give up being a minister or whatever?"

Graeme popped his knuckles. "No idea."

"Didn't he ever talk about it?"

"The odd joke now and then."

"People don't just do themselves in out of the blue."

"I wasn't all that surprised, to tell you the truth."

"No?"

"He was getting a bit seedy. They were about to sack him over at the school."

"Wasn't fooling with the kids, was he?"

"Not him, no. Had a woman friend down in Wellington, but they broke it off last year. Bugger me, I'd better ring her. Mainly he was spinning his wheels."

"We all spin our wheels. We don't all blast ourselves to kingdom come."

Graeme shrugged. Probing for motives, delving into fine points wasn't his thing. That struck me, unfairly, as a very masculine response. Feeling seedy? Just blow your head off. But it was too much for me, too. "See you in the morning," I said.

Lying awake in the dark bedroom, I listened to my heart loudly beating. I was afraid to close my eyes. All gentleness last night — after today, what? In the end I slid down the laundry chute to nothing and surfaced the next morning with no blemish of memory. At the university I gave my lecture to a lively group who seemed a lot surer than I was about where education was going in the new millennium. I had lunch in the faculty club, hugged Graeme goodbye in the tiny Sheperton airport lobby, and climbed on the feeder to Auckland.

The vision arrived just after I had strapped myself securely into seat 18A (nonsmoking, window). No memory, this — rather, a brand-new version of the forgotten six-year-old lunch unfolding in lurid Technicolour. On the other side of a patio table sat a haggard blonde angel with a smile on his face that would melt your heart. High summer, though not the summer of six years ago, lay all around us. We sipped Lemon & Paeroa straight from the bottle. Unidentifiable Antipodean insects, hordes of them, jumped crazily in the grass; I thought uneasily of biblical plagues.

He was handsome, in a high-strung sort of way. Surely the women had gone for good old Dougal McDougal, and thus, though good, could he have been so innocent? But now you would have to say he was something not quite of this world. As the hues of his skin and his hair shifted like a badly tuned television set, the vision-man looked me squarely in the eye.

I tend to be a vision doubter. "What is this about?" I asked him right away.

109

"I was never fully sure of my faith." Dougal's voice, a rich baritone with all the self-assurance of the preacher's trade, was nothing like the falsetto squeak that haunted his house. Never fully sure of his faith, he repeated, he had set it aside some years before in favour of the Gnostic doctrine as set forth in the texts of Nag Hammadi. He had become a secret believer in the world of light beyond this ravaged material world so soon to self-destruct from human folly.

It did seem like a strange conversation to be having. "So why did you kill yourself?"

"To get there faster." For a split-second the skin and hair darkened, then turned fair again. Hanging before the Throne of Glory, he explained, was a curtain of all souls that held every living creature's past and future. That's where returning souls were supposed to go. Dougal had fully expected to wind up draped in the curtain's bounteous folds, but so far he hadn't.

"The Vision of Paul says the soul of an impious man rises out of his body only to be handed over to the dreaded angel Tartaruch. That didn't happen to me either, thank God."

"What did?"

"Well, you don't find out until after you're dead that it's a rare thing for your soul to ascend all by itself. It takes outside help to blast through the wall of the seven firmaments. I keep trying and trying, but I can't escape from earth. The Archons are blocking my way." Meanwhile, he complained, he was undergoing the gradual dissolution of his living personality. Layer by layer, the psychic coating on the divine element was dissolving. "Soon the human part of me will be gone. I'll have nowhere to go but down, not up."

Dougal wrapped his arms around his body and hugged himself. Except for the colour changes, he seemed solid enough. Groups of souls, he said, came from a single root. They had special affinities and could help each other out, even in this life. He and I were so related. That's why he had come to me. "Somehow my soul just won't fly by itself. I need you to help me rise, Grace." He leaned forward urgently, causing a jerky rainbow to leap around his body. "You're my only hope. I haven't got much time. There's only forty-two days between living death and death."

"But how? How do I help you rise?"

Dougal stood up and kissed my hand. After such a speech it was a very sensual kiss. "Just leave it to me," he whispered in my ear. "Take me into you. I'll do the rest."

Something in me balked at this right away. It seemed like an overliteral way of going about things. I shook my head vigorously. What if I took him in and he couldn't, or wouldn't, get out? I remembered the buzzing voice in the living room and shivered. What if that, not the plausible vision before me, turned out to be the real Dougal? I wondered aloud — carefully avoiding the word "impious" — if possibly he had failed some test of virtue or knowledge, if he was being punished? Was there a Gnostic hell?

Dougal had an answer ready. At first — yes, he admitted it — he had had dire fears he *would* be handed over to the black angel, the lord Tartaruch, but slowly he had become convinced that this would not happen. "It's worse than that," he hissed unexpectedly, the voice suddenly taking on a familiar bitterness. "I think I've been tricked. Again! They promised my soul would leave my body, that I'd be totally free of this awful world. But I'm not. There's no escape, no gnosis. My soul belongs to my body, not to God. My blood soaked into the ground *here*."

"This is the wrong place?"

"It's where I died."

Dougal turned and walked over to the bicycle propped up against the mailbox. Just then the plane lurched forward on the runway, gathering speed, and the summer yard was gone. Shaking myself like a dog, I peered through the cramped porthole. And what do you know, there was Dougal, not bicycling but loping frantically across the patterned farmland alongside the runway.

> The hunter now has left the moor,
> The scattered coveys meet secure,
> While here I wander, prest with care,
> Along the lonely banks of Ayr.

Though he was, impossibly, keeping pace with the plane as it taxied, his struggles in the field were pitiful to watch. The harder he tried to soar, the deeper he was being sucked into the iron-red dirt — up to his ankles, up to his knees, up to his chest.

> Do not, do not leave me so!
> Do not, do not leave me so!

Again and again Dougal wrenched himself loose of the earth, plunged on after the plane.

I hadn't had the chance to ask him the question I had wanted to, which was, Why? Why should souls want to rise off the ground? Why shouldn't they just sink into it, along with their bodies? What was the fuss about, exactly? And something in me answered, Souls want to live. But help him? I shivered. There was no way, thank God. Dougal went under just as the manmade silver wings of the Air New Zealand clipper effortlessly severed me and my fellow passengers from land.

It made my heart briefly glad, this liftoff. For return ticket rates I was rising to heaven in my own body, sphere by golden sphere. Leaving Dougal way down there. Then the plane bucked sharply. We all lurched in our seats. Loud roars the wild inconstant blast, yon murky cloud is foul with rain. Yes, those treacherous South Pacific winds were back, they'd been lying in wait up here all along. My stomach rolled over. Bonnie laddie. It was going to be a bumpy flight.

Bolinas Venus

for Rupert Keenlyside

Pulling up in front of the Bolinas bakery, Sam had to swerve to avoid a long-haired man in a loincloth and down vest lying in the middle of the street. He sensed the Bolinas people eyeing him as he got out of the red Mercedes, so he left the car unlocked; he loved beating these types at their own game. Raising his hand in the "bless you" mode to Kevin, he climbed the bakery stairs, then came back with his coffee and fresh croissant to sit down heavily on the old wooden steps next to his son. There were no tables or chairs; that was typical Bolinas. Two feet away a mongrel nosed in the garbage cans.

Old Ford trucks and beat-up Chevelles and Monte Carlos cruised past the dilapidated Victorians on Wharf Road. The hip newcomers driving these cars sported bright-coloured tight pants and pompadours; cowboy New Wave, Sam supposed you'd call it. He looked over at his stoop-shouldered son, whose floppy blonde hair hung over the embroidered collar of his Mexican shirt: out of date even with his own generation. Flecks of Danish clung to the gingery wisps of Kevin's moustache. The boy had an irritating habit of gulping his food half eaten. Sam, a methodical chewer, couldn't stand to watch. "How's Rachel?" he asked finally.

Kevin choked down the rest of his pastry. "Split to L.A.," he said in a muffled voice.

"So?"

"So what?" Kevin briefly returned his father's stare, then weakened into confession. "She met this dude passing through town. He offered her this film job down there."

"I see," said Sam. Girls were always leaving Kevin. Sam himself, on the other hand, had always been the one to do the leaving. All right, Kevin's mother had kicked him out, but nowadays Sam was careful to get involved mostly on his own terms. Kevin never asked about Sam's girls. The incumbent, Merilee, was only two years older than he was.

"Where's your glasses?"

"Lost them."

"Need any money?"

Kevin hesitated. For pocket money — it was hard for Sam to picture his gentle, nearsighted son doing this, but he did — Kevin sat shotgun on local marijuana patches. Harvest time, however, was months away. Sam reached for his wallet.

"Dad," said Kevin. "Someone wants to meet you."

Sam looked up. Two flat green eyes in a solemn moon face, very close to his, stared back. The face, cruelly scored and weatherbeaten, radiated a perverse glow of innocence. The enormous middle-aged child woman stood directly in front of Sam, blocking

116

the sun. She was dressed in layers of sacking and tunic topped by a soiled down vest, the standard Bolinas ragpicker's gear.

"Meet Sonja, Dad."

With a wordless smile the woman stretched out her open palms. The air was cool in her shadow. Irrational fright gripped Sam. Hand still frozen on his wallet, he wondered if she wanted money, too.

"Sonja lives next to me in her bus. She remembers you from that time you came up to the mesa to look at Rachel's paintings."

Sam remembered the occasion — another money-generating scam — but certainly not this person. Had she perhaps been spying from the bushes? He turned back to the outstretched hands. Finally he got the message; he hadn't lived in the Bay Area this long for nothing. He laid both his palms ceremoniously over hers.

Sonja's smile increased by an order of magnitude. Her chapped, calloused paws quivered hotly in his.

"Sonja's a very holy person, Dad. She hardly ever says anything. Right now she's getting ready for her big trip. Every October her daughter Percy in Albuquerque sends her a Greyhound ticket and she goes down for the winter."

Sam looked up at Sonja. "How about that," he smiled. Giving her hands a dismissing squeeze, he tried to release them. But Sonja would not let go. Her insistent fingers grasped his even more tightly. With a shiver of disgust he could not quite hide, Sam shook her loose. He stood up. "Nice meeting you," he said pleasantly for the benefit of that unseen ironic observer he always played to. Secretly he felt like wiping his hands off on his pants. He passed some bills over to Kevin, who gave a little bob of his head and put them in his shirt pocket.

"So long, guys." Sam waved as if to a cheering crowd, then walked quickly to his car. Safely inside, he sneaked a look in the rear view mirror. Sonja had not moved. A great mute cow, she dwarfed the boy beside her. Silently the two watched Sam pull away from the curb.

Sam guided the old Mercedes along the twisting road around Bolinas Lagoon. He passed Audubon Canyon, then a few empty gulches bristling with coastal redwoods. The soft, steep folds of Mount Tamalpais were just now greening from early seasonal rain; a red-tailed hawk rode the thermal updrafts on the mountain.

Bolinas Lagoon, Sam recalled, was a very old place, part of a drowned valley marking the path of the San Andreas fault, where two massive plates of the Earth's crust grated against each other. During the last million years or so — Sam was a little vague on the dates — Bolinas and the whole Point Reyes peninsula, which were on the second plate and thus technically not even a part of the American continent, had migrated some three hundred miles up the California coast. And, as far as anybody knew, they were still heading north, at the rate of about an inch every thousand years.

And that's why they're so crazy over there in Bobo, Sam thought. It figured that his disappointing older son would live in a place like that. Bolinas was a time warp town; it boasted broke ex-rock stars, ex-New York poets, and its famous street people, wrinkled grey hobbits and trolls from the long-departed days of the Haight. In Bolinas you could still find All Species Preservation Festivals, communal solstice parties, that kind of thing.

Sam himself lived in Stinson Beach, only a stone's throw from Bolinas across the lagoon but seven miles by Highway 1. All these foggy little coastal towns north of the Golden Gate had their share of eccentrics and burnouts, but Stinson Beach was different. For one thing, it was a man's town, drawing rich commuter sportsmen and rough-and-ready ex-professionals, macho dropouts who were now carpenters, handymen, and the like. Stinson Beach people wore jeans and lots of plaid; the Fire Department and the bar were the town social centres. After the separation Sam's two other kids liked coming over Mount Tam to visit him there. Mark, a junior in high school, brought his surfboard and wet suit; Katrina liked to sit in Elwood's and pick up older men.

The roar of the surf was audible as he turned off the highway at Calle del Arroyo. The beach was a wide flat expanse lined with cottages that stretched three miles from cliff to point. Out at the point, where Sam lived, you could find fossil sand dollars. The ancient grey discs eroded out of thin shelvings of rubble, mimicking the live white sand dollars that littered the beach at low tide. Sam had a thing about the fossil sand dollars. Finding them or not finding them, he believed, was a psychic barometer of how your life was going. Just before school started, he had brought his nephew from Princeton out here. Before Sam was even able to tell the boy about clearing the mind of clutter to allow for the spontaneous, Stephen had found three perfect ones.

He pulled into the driveway of his redwood and glass beach house, the kind of place — he liked to say — where, when you walked in, you didn't know whether to buy a bottle of Scotch, deposit a check, or pray.

Sam himself had not found any fossil sand dollars for a good long while.

"What in the name of glory is *this*?" Sam called to Merilee next morning from the front door. On the mat lay a pile of twigs, some withered sour grass and purple lupine, bits of broken shell and coloured twine arranged in a matted attempt at a circle.

"A bird's nest?" she suggested, peering from behind on tiptoe with her chin resting on his shoulder in that little-girl way he detested. A wisp of her long brown hair, damp from the shower, trailed across his face.

Irritably he shrugged her off. "Are you kidding? A giant condor, maybe."

"Look, isn't that writing?"

Sam examined the sand around the pile of refuse. "No. Somebody drew it, but it's just marks. Meaningless." He stood up and surveyed the beach. The day was breaking sunny and hot. Indian summer weather. Sam looked down again. With one well-aimed kick he scattered the twigs and flowers all over the path.

"Awww," said Merilee.

"I'm going to get the paper." Planting his foot squarely in the middle of the mess, Sam launched himself off down the driveway. There's a lot of kid in me still, he thought. Merilee, he felt confident, would be watching until he got to the road.

This Sunday morning only one other person was on the path along the highway. That striking suntan, the Abercrombie and Fitch shirt — who could it be? The man got closer and Sam saw he was staggering. It was one of the derelicts who slept on the beach in the warmer months and hung around town during the day. The shirt, Sam realised with a start, was his own. He had put it in the Free Box outside the health food store only last week because the moths had gotten into it. Sam's skin prickled as the unkempt man reeled by, leaving a powerful animal smell in his wake. *His* shirt in that life. Winona had given it to him for Christmas ten years ago.

At the superette Sam bought the *Sunday Chronicle* and a loaf of whole grain bread for Merilee. Outside he paused to watch the motorcycle club from San Francisco, a group of middle-class, heterosexual professionals in black leather, roar through town on their weekly jaunt to Point Reyes. Frank the banker stood next to him in Levis, running shoes, and raggedy T-shirt. Over the noise he yelled in Sam's ear, "Going to the wedding?" Sam raised his eyebrows. "The wedding," Frank repeated. "Tina and Bob. Over at the Community Centre." Sam laughed and shook his head. Bob was a plumber's helper and Tina was the waitress at the little breakfast place. Stinson Beach was supposed to be an egalitarian sort of town where everybody went to everybody else's social does. Sam did show up now and then, wearing his ironic smile, but he was goddamned if he was going to invite the town riffraff to his private parties and he knew more than a few others who felt the same way.

Suddenly he ducked behind the shelter of the superette veranda. "What's with you?" said Frank. Now that the motorcycles were well up the highway, his voice rang out too loudly.

"Take a look down the road and tell me what you see."

Frank looked. "Oh, my God," he laughed. "You've got to get used to that around here. It's not like you to be squeamish, Sam."

"I don't want her to see me." As soon as Sam said it, he wished he hadn't.

Frank guffawed. "What's the matter? Broken romance?" He cupped his hands and shouted. "Hey, Sonja!"

"Shut up!" Sam whispered fiercely.

But the Bolinas woman did not hear. Attended by three mangy dogs, she walked dreamily along the road. Even from this distance Sam could see the clouds of fleas swarming over the little group; that would be from the natural eucalyptus button flea collars, he thought. Sonja had shed her gypsy gear this balmy day in favour of a crocheted string bikini and ancient rubber thongs. Unclothed, her ample body had the texture of an old leather bag with hundreds of golf balls rolling around loosely inside. The macramé had stretched impossibly to contain the sway of her long, pendulous breasts.

"What's the name of that prehistoric statue they dug up in Germany or wherever it was?" said Frank. "You know, the lumpy one without the face?"

Sam did not reply. Sonja had crossed the intersection by the gas station without looking their way. Her broad rear and the frowsy butts of the three dogs wagged purposefully toward the other end of town.

"Where could she be heading?" the banker wondered. "You hardly ever see Sonja on this side of the lagoon." But Sam barely heard him. He was gone, walking firmly home in the opposite direction.

That night at Elwood's, Sam and his cronies had gathered in their down vests and jeans to play liar's dice when Frank came up. Sam thought he had never seen such an offensive smirk.

"Hey, Sam, your girlfriend got herself arrested."

"Merilee?" said one of the others, incredulous but eager. Stinson Beachers lived on gossip.

"Sonja," said Frank. It seemed to Sam there was a small stir. "She picked a fight with the Maid of Honour at the reception. Pushed Mary right in the drainage ditch, outfit and all. They called the sheriff. Sonja's in the cooler now."

"New ladylove?" someone said. They all knew how proud Sam was of his slender young women.

An ominous red flush gathered in the wattles of Sam's neck, but he kept on shaking the box. "My throw, gentlemen." He threw.

Two days later, Sonja was out of jail and back in Stinson Beach. Reports of her, Sam knew, filtered among the townspeople. Already a few alert ears had picked up Frank's comment and ripples were coming back to Sam. Someone spotted Sonja leaving a wilted dandelion under the windshield wiper of the Mercedes when he parked it at the gas station.

The town was primed to Sonja's presence and waiting to see what would happen.

Then one evening Sam met her — and not by accident, he suspected. It was early dusk on the path by the highway. Fully clothed, she blocked his way. Dogs lapped around her ankles in little waves. Locking Sam in that disturbing blank gaze of hers — drug psychosis, he wondered, or congenital retardation? — she said nothing. When he brusquely attempted to pass, Sonja stepped only slightly aside on the narrow trail, obliging Sam to brush against the edge of her filthy down vest. Then, a few paces behind, she began to follow him.

They were almost to the street light at the highway. It would be the end, Sam thought, if anybody saw them. He turned on her and stamped his foot angrily. "Go away!" The lack of control in his voice shocked him. He stamped his foot again. "Quit following me!"

"Look," he said finally, "what do you want?" Out-and-out appeasement, but for Sonja this seemed to be the password. Immediately she raised her arms in the air and swayed back and forth on the dark path. Oh, brother, Sam thought. Incantation time. I'll let her do whatever she wants and maybe she'll go away. Except go down on me, he amended quickly, I won't let her do that. No, sir. He pictured the act and shuddered.

But Sonja's intent seemed directed elsewhere. Eyes closed, she swayed and moaned, shifting from side to side with her eyes closed. Once she stepped on a dog, which let out a piercing yelp. Then she stopped dancing and began grunting. Grunt, grunt,

grunt! Before Sam knew what to think, she had bent over and lifted her skirts, revealing her big bare ass. As Sam stared dumbfounded, Sonja farted in his face. Then, with a coarse, experienced laugh that held more of the barroom than the asylum, she dropped her skirts and sped off into the night.

Sam stood very still, the acrid odour lingering in his nostrils. Then, head down, he walked quickly toward town. In his mind the image of those two pale buttocks, a pair of blind fat worms, loomed mocking and triumphant.

Next morning another small pile of detritus lay on the doorstep. Sam, who had lifted his foot automatically, paused a long moment. Had last night been punishment for disturbing the first morning's offering? Lips tightening, he aimed carefully and let fly. The lupine and nasturtiums sailed through the air, some landing near the scattered remains of the previous week. He walked back into the kitchen, where his cup of coffee sat steaming on the table. When he had first gone to the front door, Sam realised, he had been checking. And had been right. Jesus.

Merilee was watching him. "What's the matter?"

"Nothing." He wished he had picked up all the little bits on the step so she wouldn't see them when she went out. Maybe there was still time if she went to the bathroom.

But Merilee was absorbed in other things. "I'm so excited, Sam," she cried, hugging herself. She had on a smart knit ensemble, rose coloured, plus stockings and high heels. Today was the first day of her new job selling real estate. Sam didn't like the looks of the guy in the white Porsche who had given her the job even before she had sat for the real estate exam. Merilee was supposed to be his trainee. Trainee. Sam had never seen her out of jeans before.

"Good luck," he said casually, sipping his coffee. Sam felt he had a better chance of keeping his girls if he always seemed slightly bored.

"I'm so nervous," Merilee said. Her heels clicked as she disappeared toward the back for a last session with the mirror. Sam jumped up and ran to the front door. He brushed the remaining twigs and silver foil off the step and was back in his seat by the time Merilee reappeared. She leaned over to give him a kiss. "See you tonight." Sam smiled briefly.

The wheels of Merilee's Honda Civic crunched in the gravel outside as Sam chewed his toast thoughtfully. After his wife had left him — or rather, made him move out — Sam had evolved a definite credo about his involvements. Before, while he was married, they were informal, spontaneous, passionate. Now that he was, so to speak, unprotected, his new arrangements had become as formal as a Japanese tea ceremony, to wit:

1. No love talk, no plighting of troth.
2. No visiting of relatives (the parents of his girls were likely to be the same age or younger than Sam).
3. No questioning about the other person's outside activities (though Sam as a matter of course broke off with the girl if he found she had slept with someone else; he personally was not interested in being laughed at).

Finally, Sam's mood swings, which were frequent and severe for such a deliberate person, were to be tolerated without comment or complaint. Resistance or — God forbid — attempts at manipulation were completely unacceptable.

These requirements demanded a fairly regular switch of partners to keep up the standard, but so far, except for one regrettable experience with a French girl in which Sam had almost forgotten himself, he had no complaints about his setup, which left his heart free and clear for the real woman he would someday meet, though probably not at Elwood's — the sophisticated beauty somewhere between the ages of 28 and 35 who would see through this facade, love Sam, forgive him, and keep him up to the mark. He would take her on that special trip to Europe he had been planning over the years. When they were in Paris he would wear his suit from Wilkes Bashford and she would wear a hat with a little black veil — no, of course she wouldn't wear such a thing, that was stuff from his own prehistory, but he liked imagining it anyway.

Meanwhile the long-legged girls in jeans would do very well, the willowy ones, idealistic, with a big father thing. It was risky — they were so fickle, and often incredibly boring — but he needed those clear eyes, that fresh complexion, the unquestioning approval. Meeting the shrewd, worldly, bitter gaze of a woman of his own years and class in an intimate setting was about as enticing a prospect to Sam as an unflushed toilet.

He took another sip of coffee. This real estate situation would have to be carefully monitored; if necessary, Sam would time a suitable breakaway. There was a girl he ran into occasionally at the post office who seemed possible, but he thought he had heard someone tell him she was crazy. There were a lot of crazies in this sheltered West Marin environment. Sometimes they came across normal at first: closet crazies. He would have to do some serious checking.

Meanwhile Winona, through her lawyer who was incidentally an old friend of Sam's, had just put through a demand for $850,000 up front. Safely ensconced in the family abode in Ross, wrapped in the warm cloak of her grievances, she sent these directives over the mountain to Sam who, like some pagan god of money, was supposed to wave his wand and cause this sum to materialise in her (now separate) bank account. How had she arrived at this figure? Sam knew how. By Winona's reckoning, it would add up to about a dime per hurt. Sam was supposed to feel punished, guilty, *bad*. And pay for it. That was the whole point, blood money. Winona had money of her own. She just wanted to get him. That familiar female Gestapo ultimatum, disguised as "feelings" but just as transparent as the morning pile of doorstep crud: Love me or you're going to get it.

Well, Sam couldn't be gotten. Not that way. The angry knot inside him tightened another full twist. Sure, Winona, $850,000 — take it, you got it. Better me earning it than you or we'd have a long wait, wouldn't we?

As expected, Merilee came home full of her new job and the witty sayings of her boss Tom, a prize asshole by the sound of it. Here you had the big problem with father complexes — the mantle of godhood seemed to fit such a large number of men. To get away from the Tom-this and Tom-that and maybe explore the possibilities of the post office girl, Sam fled the house. That night and the next, he walked warily down the path to Elwood's. No one appeared to block his way; the expected trailside retribution never came. The morning offerings had also stopped. Sam felt relieved, though not without a twinge of ego. Even the crazies are fickle, he thought.

The third night Elwood's was packed. Sam had just eased himself into a chair near the Franklin stove when a group of people directly in front of him broke up, revealing a large woman sitting at the bar. Even with her back to him, Sam had no difficulty recognising Sonja. Quickly he got up and moved to the far end of the bar.

Sonja, hunched over her drink, seemed oblivious. As nearly as one could make out, the Bolinas woman was depressed. Her tanned jowls drooped, the eyes looked more than usually glazed. Under the inevitable down vest, Sam noticed, she wore the remnants of a gauzy Indian dress. This parody of feminine attire reminded him that he had actually heard of this woman long before last week. Vague stories that she had once been married to a lawyer, had children, grown children, somewhere. Sam tried, and failed, to imagine Sonja making their school lunches. Somewhere along the line, perhaps during the psychedelic madness, the fairies had spirited away the lawyer's wife, leaving this changeling in her place.

Sonja's drink was a fancy cocktail, a Pimm's cup or something like it — poignant echo of a bourgeois past, Sam wondered? Sonja, like all the other West Marin heavies, would undoubtedly be on medication — thorazine, stelazine, or some exotic combination thereof. She probably ought not to be drinking at all. Sam was about to mention this to the bartender but stopped himself. That would clinch it. All those watching eyes would note that Sam was taking care of "his girl." Screw it. The yellow skin, for all its cellulite slackness, looked tough and battle scarred. Sonja had already survived, if not very well, some fifty-odd years without his assistance.

Sam fell into conversation with the man next to him, a retired naval officer who was now a chimney sweep in Point Reyes Station. When he glanced over in Sonja's direction again, the stool was empty, the Pimm's cup with its soggy lemon a melted ruin on the bar. Sam cast a nervous look over his shoulder. She was nowhere in the room.

Later, walking home under the frosty stars, he felt his shoulders brace protectively — against the cold? But he reached his dark house unmolested.

Crawling into bed Sam fell determinedly on Merilee's thin gangly body — licked it, devoured it, then gave it a thorough what-for. Except for an occasional moan Merilee said nothing the whole time and rolled over on her back at precisely the same moment Sam rolled over on his. A split-second later, catapulted into dreamland, he found himself wandering through a barren landscape. Not wandering, searching. He was on some kind of mission, in this desert of rolling hills that were not exactly sand dunes. The object of his quest was unclear, but the frustration attached to it was not. He had been thwarted for lifetimes. Eternities. Failure had become an enduring condition he had built his life around. But now there was a sense of hidden excitement. Something momentous was about to happen. He stood on the edge of a deep pit, looking down. There was something in the bottom of the pit, curled up like a snail. Then this object was moving rapidly toward Sam — or was Sam himself falling into the pit? Panic mounted, but he could do nothing to prevent the converging of himself with she who could not be named, this enormous, grossly naked woman in flexed position, flesh smeared with red ochre, looking more like a giant lizard than a human, eyes closed but oh, God! if they should open —

Sam's own eyes flew wide apart. He lay on the designer sheets next to Merilee, heart pounding furiously. Still half in the dream, his mind pored over its details. The dusky red of her skin. The objects arranged around her body — black, shiny, sinister. And Sam was supposed to be doing something. He was supposed to be — *not* touching those objects. Definitely not. He shivered at the thought. And the eye, the one visible eye. If it had winked opened — and it had been just about to, Sam knew for certain — then what would have happened?

Sam jumped out of bed and put on his robe against the chill. He walked into the dark kitchen and sat down at the table. A crescent moon shone in the window. On the beach, over the crashing waves, a dog howled. Sam sat in darkness for a long time. How long he didn't know. When he finally glanced over at the luminous dial of the stove clock, it was

131

half past four. He had not been thinking about anything much; it had been, he supposed, a kind of
trance. Sam got up. He went back into the bedroom
and climbed in next to Merilee, bolt awake, awaiting
sunrise.

In the next few weeks Sam's life took a turn for the
worse. For starters, he couldn't perform. At first
Merilee had smothered him in sticky understanding. When nothing changed, she subsided into
puzzled hurt and now, Sam fancied, a certain child-
like indifference, though she still came home
promptly after work and cooked dinner like a good
girl. Night after night he tried. No luck. Once
Merilee gravely suggested counselling. "*Ther*-apee,"
he mocked, then brought her off with his mouth.
But who was he kidding?

Smells haunted him. Odors of fish, rotten leaves,
dead animals filled his nostrils, even when he was
safe in his office in the City. He thought about
translucent membranes, blue veins, dogs smacking
their chops as they ate the placenta of their pups,
thin watery menstrual fluid.

After one more night of disaster, Sam got up early
and trudged down the beach. He could hear the
salmon boats right outside the shorebreak but
couldn't see them; the sun lay inside a giant fogbank
like a heavy, moist pearl. Transparent jellyfish the
size of dinner plates were scattered on the beach.
There were tangles of kelp, orange rinds, Clorox
bottles, the matted feathers of dead seagulls. A flock
of reptilian-looking pelicans cruised low overhead.

Sam walked and walked. At the end of the beach

he sat down on a rotten piece of timber. The ocean lapped listlessly against the ugly grey sand; a bad tidal smell rose off the lagoon. Directly across the channel the frame houses of Bolinas floated ghost-like over the river of fog.

Sam tapped his foot rhythmically — like a horny teenager, he realised, and stopped. But not before his toe had struck something hard in the sand. He scratched around and there it was, waiting for him. Elated, he cupped the fossil sand dollar in his palm.

A sensation overwhelmingly cold and imper-sonal rose from the petrified shell with its shirred five-pointed star pattern. Sam pocketed the fossil and got to his feet. Feeling better than he had in a long time, he strode briskly back down the beach, skin tingling from the prickly dampness of the fog. He whistled as he slammed the front door and lifted his eyebrows to Merilee in ironic greeting. Why strain to prove a point? Tonight he would show her.

By mid-morning his elation had faded. Merilee had gone to work, then phoned back an hour later to say she wouldn't be home for dinner. The fog con-gealed into rain. Sam paced impatiently, tapping the sand dollar in his pocket through the heavy fabric of his pants. His energy was back, the luck (he hoped) was back, too. What to do with it? Stuck in this god-forsaken boring little town, shacked up with a girl barely out of her teens in a beach house with sink-ing foundations. Sam slammed out the door and jumped into the Mercedes. The back tire whirled monotonously in a patch of mud, then skidded free. He was off.

The rain had slackened when he pulled up at the superette. Two or three of the regulars lounging outside the entrance exchanged glances as Sam got out of his car. He ignored them. When he came back out with his Chronicle, Timmy, a burly wastrel and son of his lawyer friend Roger, beckoned him over. Noting the open Coors in Timmy's hand, Sam glanced at his watch — ten thirty in the morning. His unspoken judgment did not faze Timmy, who grinned broadly. "You made the headlines, Sam!" he shouted. The others sniggered.

Sam started, looking down at his paper. "Not there," Timmy said. "Here." He pointed up at the side of the superette, where an enormous heart ten feet high had been crudely spray-painted in indelible red:

**SAM
LOVES
SONJA**

Sam gaped. Then, realising he was being watched, he swallowed quickly and tried again. "Which of you jokers is responsible for this?" That was not what he had intended to say. The menace in his voice made them laugh even harder. "Assholes," he muttered. Spinning on his heel, he jumped into his car — exactly the wrong, uncool reaction, the tireless observer inside him noted. As he roared off, Sam just had time to hear one of the fellows reciting the old jumprope rhyme: "First comes love, then comes marriage, then comes Sam and Sonja with a baby carr..."

Sam did the lagoon road at something faster than his usual pace. He took the unmarked turnoff to Bolinas on two wheels and gunned through town without slowing down. When he got to the Day-Glo painted mailbox on the mesa road, he turned onto the bumpy dirt driveway that led to Kevin's and pulled up beside the converted barn with a squeal of brakes.

His son sat on the rusted carcass of a wheelbarrow, deeply engrossed in a task Sam could not quite make out. Surprise showed on Kevin's face as he looked up. "Dad," he said simply.

"Hi," Sam returned curtly through the car window. Now that he was here, he could think of no plausible reason for his visit. Kevin, he now saw, was whittling a long wooden dowel blank. Out of habit Sam needled him. "I thought you didn't believe in killing God's creatures."

"The deer eat all our vegetables. We hunt them to save our crops and because their natural predators are gone." It sounded like a speech Kevin had made a lot.

"Very commendable," said Sam.

By that curious second sight of sons Kevin seemed to sense his father's confusion. "Why don't you get out of the car?" he said reasonably and Sam, to his own astonishment, obeyed. He walked over and sat down on a redwood burl. Kevin picked up a formidable bow, hand carved, and bent it between his legs. The effort made the tendons leap out in his narrow arms. "This is the way I string the bow," he said patiently, as if he were talking to a child, and Sam nodded. He watched Kevin's hands move over the bow and realised with a sense of wonder that there were a few areas of life — terribly limited ones, of

135

course — in which his older son had managed to achieve a kind of competence. They sat pleasantly side by side while Kevin worked. It was Kevin, however, who broke the silence. "When did you take it?"

Sam was puzzled. "Take what?"

His son shot him a shrewd look. "What you're high on."

"I'm not high on anything." Sam felt impatient. The mood was spoiled; he was starting to become his old self again and Kevin had turned back into a fool.

But this time Kevin did not respond to the unconscious cue. His shoulders did not hunch over protectively, his eyes did not drop to the ground. He kept at his work without the slightest sign of concern. Sam realised with alarm that his son had not believed him. His hand shot into his pocket and fingered the sand dollar for reassurance. Fat lot of good it's done me so far, he thought.

Kevin indicated a narrow goat track that ran behind the barn. "Sonja lives up there."

Sam started. "Now hold on."

Whittling again, Kevin did not look up.

"Did you hear what I said?" Sam paused. "I said, hold on. I want to know why you said that. Do you hear me?"

"Said what?" said Kevin,

Sam made an exasperated noise. "You know what. Don't play dumb with me. *Why* did you say it? That's what I want to know."

Kevin's attention was absorbed in the exquisite point he was putting on his dowel blank. Flick, flick! went the knife. Fighting the impulse to kick him across the barnyard, Sam took a deep breath. "What

136

have people been saying to you, Kevin? Please tell me that, please."

Kevin looked up. He was genuinely puzzled, Sam saw. "I don't know what you mean, Dad. What are people supposed to be saying?"

"I want to know what made you bring up this woman Sonja. What made you mention her out of left field like that."

Kevin's mother's small blue eyes shone up guilelessly at Sam. "Well, because you met her the other week when we were at the bakery, that's why. I don't know why I said it. It just seemed like something to say."

Sam let out his breath. "All right. Never mind." He got up and paced around the yard. Kevin was watching him closely, he realised. Speculating, as he rested the arrow on his forearm and sighted it in Sam's direction. Well, screw him. Kevin might think he was getting one up on his old Dad at last but Sam could take up the reins any time he wanted, no problem. It was just that right now —

Kevin dropped the arrow and rushed over to him. "Dad, what's the matter?" His curried breath, that crap his food cooperative ate for breakfast, brought Sam back from wherever he had just gone. Shaken, he got to his feet, brushing off Kevin's attempts to help him. He had fallen to the ground in a kind of faint, it seemed. There was mud all over the seat of his new blue jeans and the creeping dampness had already hit his buttocks. "No, no, no," Sam said to every query of Kevin's as he strode to the car and jumped in. He started the engine and let out the clutch; Kevin had to leap back to get his foot out from under the rolling wheels as Sam took off.

A new downpour of rain began as he reached the intersection of the driveway and the mesa road. Water gushed from the sky; the wipers could barely clear the windshield. Hands shaking slightly on the wheel, Sam crept along the road. The concentration took his mind off what had just happened, though he wasn't exactly sure what *had* happened. Gaining confidence, he picked up speed. Around a steep bend a large uprooted tree blocked the road. He slammed on the brakes. The car spun straight across the glassy surface of the road like a shot bolt. There was a tremendous impact; Sam felt a sudden suffocation.

When he came to again — was it minutes or hours later? — he was not slumped over the steering wheel but in motion, walking purposefully up the road. Where am I headed? Sam asked his goal-oriented body. The Day-Glo mailbox, it answered. Kevin. Sam gave in without a murmur — it seemed like a good idea and besides, his head ached horri-bly — but a few minutes later he was forced to admit that he had either overshot the mailbox or was headed in the wrong direction. He stopped, feeling dizzy and strange. If only a car would come by. Resisting the impulse to sit down in the middle of the road, he walked over to the shoulder. Here was a side road of sorts — not Kevin's road, but still a road. Surely someone lived at the end, even though the rutted dirt track did not look as if it had been recently used. Sam hesitated, then started up it. I'll give this a hundred yards, he decided sensibly.

The track wound through one of those messy eucalyptus groves that molted leaves and bark all year round. Mist straggled through the treetops; water dripped through the bare branches onto Sam's head. The underbrush was alive with scurryings, unexplained clicking noises. A dismal place, he thought, keeping his eyes on the track.

Still looking down at his feet, Sam rounded a bend and walked straight into the back of an enormous vehicle. Stunned, he reeled to one side. It was an ancient yellow school bus heeled slightly over in the earth like a sailboat catching the wind. Painted in black on one side were the letters TAMALPAIS UNION HIGH SCHOOL. All four enormous tires were flat, their rusty rims deeply settled in the earth. Next to the bus lay the dead remains of a campfire; around it sprawled a pack of dogs too enervated to challenge Sam. A persistent sound of croaking came from a nearby mud pond covered with lily pads. An occasional pad popped up like a tea kettle lid. Tiny eyes regarded Sam.

I shouldn't be here, he thought suddenly, feeling an overwhelming impulse to run. Too late. A strong hand clamped onto his shoulder. "Oh no," Sam groaned aloud. Slowly he turned back around to face those implacable eyes.

Sonja did not look at all surprised to see him. She raised her hand casually to the scruff of his neck. Sam's knees buckled as she hauled him onto the bus like a wayward puppy.

Force-marched down the narrow aisle, Sam felt his gorge rise at the rich assortment of smells — damp rot, incense, cat piss, the musk of a female animal's den. Sonja laid him out on a filthy piece of bare foam — her bed, he realised — and dragged a stained sleeping bag over him. Sam submitted without a struggle. The will to resist had deserted him. He was cold and tired and needed to rest. Who cared if the sleeping bag stank a little? He could handle this. Let her take care of him, let him catch his breath. Soon he'd slip away and no one would be the wiser about this accidental tête-a-tête. A fleeting worry about the Mercedes scudded through his brain. Where was it, in what kind of shape? Wrapped around a madrone tree, some part of him replied. People would start searching for him, but not for a while; the car was still registered to Winona's address.

Sonja lit a Primus stove in the driver's seat. Heating some water for him, Sam guessed. The old training died hard. This thought produced a strained chuckle. Pieces of corrugated cardboard and tattered bits of fabric were draped over the cloudy, fly-specked windows. Half the seats were torn out; the other half were stacked with cardboard boxes full of junk, rusted-out car batteries, pieces of rubber tubing, stacks of yellowed newspapers. As far as Sam could see, there was no source of heat in the bus other than the portable stove she was now pumping. He shivered under the ruined sleeping bag. Jesus, the woman was hardy.

Soon a cracked mug of steaming liquid appeared under his nose. Herbal tea, Ovaltine of the hip. He propped himself up awkwardly on one elbow. Now that he had stopped moving, every bone in his body ached. Avoiding her eyes, he took the mug from Sonja. Broken springs creaked as she sat down in the seat opposite his pallet. She was, he sensed, staring down at him. Like a great patient cow. Beneath his shock and fatigue Sam felt irritation rising. If there was one thing that bugged him, it was people — women — hovering around. With an angry motion he waved her away.

The next moment tea was all over Sam's jacket and his face burned from a stinging crack of the hand. It took him a moment to put it together. Sonja had *hit* him. His nose was bleeding from the blow. He looked at her in amazement. Back in her seat across from him, placid as ever, Sonja did not seem upset. Sam began struggling to his feet. This would not do, it would simply not do. He was going to have to leave a little sooner than he was ready to, it seemed. Immediately Sonja rose and pushed him flat on his back, knocking the breath out of him.

As he lay gasping, a *National Enquirer*-type headline flashed across Sam's brain: "Madwoman's Sex Prisoner Held Hostage in Bus." Then a subhead: "Middle-Aged Broker Forced to Perform Unspeakable Acts." Then a smudgy wire press photo: a weeping Sam, shielding his face with his hands, led away by police for sex abuse counselling, a handcuffed Sonja flashing a triumphant grin to the popping of flashbulbs. Hadn't there been a movie like this once? Only a girl victim, of course. In a basement or something.

Sam decided to speak. "I thought you *liked* me."

Looking down at him, Sonja appeared to consider this statement. In the dark schoolbus her impassive face was cast in shadow. But even in broad daylight, Sam felt, he could not have read her expression. He watched the movement of her enormous chest in and out, in and out, under the bulky layers of Free Box

141

clothing. Sonja's body odour alone, dense and rank, made him forget he had ever smelled anything pleasant or fresh. Something clawed at his foot. Sam screamed. An ancient black and white tomcat, one eye milky and blind, the other half hidden under a drooping eyelid, with a neck muscular as a prizefighter's, was creeping up Sam's body to join his mistress. Sonja's free hand reached down absently to pet it. The hideous creature let out a loud ragged noise like a diesel engine, full of sputtering and misfires.

Helpless, staring up at her and the cat, Sam felt the full force of Sonja's silent attention. Just as he had feared, once he started looking into those green eyes he could not look away; like a fly struggling on the surface of a pool, he did not want to be drawn under. But he was fascinated, too. That deeply etched female face seemed to open up something wonderful and sad inside Sam. The hand pushing down on his chest kept him mired in this muck, this terrible pain and joy. Sam wanted no part of it, good or bad; he wanted to be free. He struggled again, horrified at how weak he had grown. Sonja's arm was pinning him to the earth; the massive trunk seemed to grow straight out of his heart. But there was something even stranger: though her face was as weatherbeaten as the redwood siding on Sam's house, the skin on the inside of Sonja's arms was not. It was soft, unmarked. Luminous, even. More than anything in the world he wanted to touch it.

Sonja did not stop his tentative hand as it brushed against the wondrous skin. Or his cheek as he slowly raised up and laid his head against her arm. Waves of dancing light zigzagged through him, lifting him up. He felt like a bubble of champagne rising to the top of the glass.

With a jolt Sam came to his senses, thinking: I'm crouched inside a squalid schoolbus nuzzling this stinking bag of fat. He made a convulsive movement toward the door. Sonja pushed him down again. This time a new feeling possessed Sam. He was dying. A heart attack, shock, exposure from the accident — whatever the cause, he was "passing on." On Bolinas mesa. In a derelict's bed. "No, no, no," he whispered. Sonja's face now seemed fixed in the firmament a million miles above him. Desperately Sam looked up at her for some sign of pity. But there was nothing in those merciless sky-eyes watching his pathetic struggles way down here. Sam was plunged into despair. Nothing seemed left to do except the thing he now did. "Kevin," he called softly, without hope. "Kevin, help me."

As soon as he said this, some constricted thing within Sam released itself. Rapidly a series of changes unfolded inside him; it was as if his very cells were mutating. Under Sonja's hand his body rippled and heaved through a roller-coaster metamorphosis. And the new, emerging Sam wanted something. What did he want?

Sonja.

Abruptly the shaking stopped. All was still. From her impossible height Sonja lowered herself to Sam, who shut his eyes in terror and joy. He knew the moment of consummation — his death — had come. There was a pause, a hiccup of silence. Then two human lips pressed softly against his in a delicate kiss.

A rich sensation of pleasure flooded Sam's breast. Slowly he opened his eyes. "That's all?" he said incredulously. "Just a kiss?"

Sonja's face was close to his. Now her eyes were warm and green, filled with a joyous love light. Sam basked in it. Though her arm was off his chest, he still felt pierced through and through.

"Sam loves Sonja," she said. It was not a question.

Sam rose humbly from the bed. Awkwardly, because the aisle was so narrow and full of junk, he dropped to one knee and kissed the splayed dirty foot before him. "Sam loves Sonja," he said, eyes full of tears. It was the noblest moment of his life.

Outside the schoolbus night had fallen. Feeling silly and wonderful, clothes torn and dirty but soul feather light, Sam loped down the darkening path, vaulting logs like a graceful buck. Sonja had set him free, the free-est he had ever known, but it was the oddest sensation: he felt he had the strength of four legs, not two.

When he came out of the eucalyptus grove, Sam was not on the mesa road, as he had expected to be. Instead he stood on a small rise overlooking an enormous red roof. With a shock he realised he had come out behind Kevin's barn. Surefooted Sam galloped down the twisting dirt path but hesitated, suddenly shy, outside the front door. Prowling around the side of the barn, he came to an unshaded window and peeked in. In the twilit room Kevin lay asleep on a bare mattress, dirty sheets twisted under him. The strung bow lay at the foot of the bed next to a sheaf of homemade arrows. But Kevin was not altogether

Kevin. Inhabiting his son Sam saw a powerful spirit, the mingled essence of Winona and himself, a radiant winged being whose luminous exhalations filled the shabby room with light. Kevin had been conceived in love. Sam had forgotten that simple fact — if, indeed, he had ever realised it at all.

Removing his clothes, he sank to his knees in the heavy undergrowth. He knelt outside the shining room a long time. Then he got up and began to walk, very fast, down the driveway to the mesa road. He had to get home, had to get back to Stinson Beach. Then he thought of Merilee and stopped dead in his tracks. What was he to do about Merilee? He tried to picture her face, but all he could see in his mind's eye was her slender body, which seemed wrong. Then he watched the body turn from very young to very old. The creature "Merilee" became a skeletal hag. He could see the bones under the skin, the once-firm flesh withered into sinews. In a moment he would raise his eyes to the skull —

Sam was shaking his head to dispel the vision as a set of headlights swung around the next curve. He waved frantically. The old Volkswagen stopped a little past him, exhaust chugging, taillights glowing ruby red in the dusk. He ran up to the driver's side and said it.

"Sam loves Sonja!"

The young couple inside regarded him. Without speaking, they rolled up their windows in unison and pushed down the door locks. The car rumbled off.

Choking in the exhaust, Sam thought: they must be from Stinson Beach. A saying popped into his head. Love laughs at locksmiths. He laughed, too. Around the next bend the wreckage of the red Mercedes appeared. Yes, it had been a madrone. Sam passed by without a second glance. He had to hurry, hurry, set things right while he could still see it all so clearly. Just wait till I tell them at Elwood's, he exulted.

It was dark now, dark as only a country road can be. Overhead the torrent of stars flowed like a river. The brightest star lit up the cloud tops over Duxbury Reef, spilling light onto the Bolinas cliffs, the shaggy treetops, even the cracked pavement of the road. Sam stopped in wonder. The evening star had risen to guide his ignorant feet through the darkness; she would lead Sam safely home. Poised trustfully, he drew a breath. Then he rushed eagerly down her glittering, crooked path.

Agony brought him awake — the excruciating sensation of being flayed and burned alive, of millions of tiny ants biting his body. The pain grew past bearability. He bellowed in anguish and woke himself up.

At the first rush of sights and sounds — too-bright sunlight, seashell-patterned sheets, the muffled roar of crashing waves — he thought: what well-lit corner of hell have they put me in? Then someone touched him. Sam screamed.

"Calm down," a girl's unsympathetic voice said. "I have to put some more Calomel lotion on you."

Merilee? Sam jerked his head around. To his relief she looked the same as always, though incredibly young: that light brown hair, the unlined child's face. What had he been expecting? A new wave of torment swept his body. He looked down and saw to his horror that it was he, not Merilee, who had been transformed. Sam now wore some unholy creature's bright red bumpy skin, covered with a disgusting milky crust that broke and ran in spots. "What happened?" he moaned.

Gently but impatiently Merilee was rubbing a thick liquid into his arm. Her lips pursed in disapproval. "You rolled around in some poison oak, I guess."

"Oh, Jesus." Though it hurt incredibly, he turned to look at her again. Why was she so mad? His memory was blank — or rather, it was a whirl of disturbing images that seemed to have very little to do with his present position in time and space. He remembered the schoolbus — oh, yes — but little else. "How did I get here?"

"You showed up naked at Elwood's. They called me to come take you home."

Sam digested this information. In a calm voice he asked, "What else did I do?"

"What else, you jerk? What do you mean, what else? Oh, you wrecked your car, too. They were all out searching for you."

Even in anger Merilee's face was child-like — though she had sounded there, for a moment, alarmingly like Winona. Sam stared at her, fascinated. She was — she hasn't even been *born* yet, he thought. Like I have. For some reason it made him think of how Katrina's hair stood straight up when she was a baby, as if she had seen a ghost.

But Merilee had just called him a "jerk." That had been uncommonly bold of her. Now she was saying, "You want to know what else you did? You — "

"Please give me the phone," Sam croaked. The itching had abated enough for him to realise he had a severe head cold. Wordlessly Merilee handed him the receiver. Sam punched the buttons with his monster's fingers. Buzz, buzz, then a voice. "Kevin," Sam said.

"Dad, Dad, what happened to you? The car — "

"I'm all right. Don't worry. Listen, son, I've got to tell you two things. Number one, I love you. Number two, can you get a message to Sonja?"

There was a short silence on the other end. Then Kevin said, "Sonja's gone to her daughter's. She hitchhiked out early this morning."

"I see," said Sam. "Well, you take it easy, son. Goodbye." He put down the receiver. Merilee looked at him without curiosity and said, "As soon as I get another layer of this gunk all over you, I've got to go. Tom and I are showing houses today."

A cushioned pang, like a bell tolling underwater, rang through Sam's ravaged body. Of course the fellow was now Merilee's lover. Amazing how unmistakably he could sense it. He could also see the broken bits of plaster where his own image had fallen and shattered in her good but unformed heart. The young animal in this one was stronger than the tender feelings. This one, in fact, did not really love him and so perhaps — perhaps — he had not been so disgraceful to her after all. But some of the others, one or two he had sent away — he could summon those faces easily now and see that precious light shining —

Tears sprang to his eyes. Looking uncomfortable, Merilee let go his hand and got up. She thought Sam was upset about her, he saw. "See you later," she said, clicking out the door. High heels again. Ah, the exhilaration of being the winner, the one in amatory control — how well Sam knew it. He almost smiled to see how cocky, how energetic, the prospect made her. Her new friend Tom would notice that special aura and he, too, would be ensnared. A few heartbeats later, Sam heard the Honda roll jauntily out of the driveway, spitting gravel.

Alone now, he struggled out of bed. Barely able to keep from falling to the floor in a frenzy of scratching, he managed to wrap a towel loosely around his swollen body. He shuffled to the patio door and let himself out onto the beach. Waves pounded brightly on the bare sand. Sand dollars — live ones — lay everywhere; the ocean had brought them up overnight. Up the coast, beyond the end of the spit, Bolinas shimmered in the salt spray mist. Sam stared a long time at those white cliffs, the ones that, four hundred years ago, had reminded Sir Francis Drake of Dover and caused him to dub this land Nova Albion, the ones that still lit up like mirrors every afternoon from the rays of the sinking sun.

Sam believed in cutting your losses. His skin would heal. The Mercedes would get a new front end. That big red — *design* on the superette wall would fade in a couple of years — though he would still have to leave town, of course. But the great event itself was settling into place at the centre of his heart with the same disturbing permanence as that elusive presence just now peeking over the mesa — the evening star that was also the morning star, palely receded, yet undeniably present, in the greater luminosity of the daytime sky. Sam loved Sonja. With pounding heart, one puffy hand clutching his bath towel, he watched her start to rise.

Also Available in this Series

THE NIGHT SINGERS by Valerie Miner
160 pages, 0 907123 899, £7

Valerie Miner's stories consider the fluctuating definitions of family and friendship, with wit, compassion and literary grace, paying attention to geographical place and historical moment. In a small New England town a gay man and his lesbian friend explore varieties of sexual intimacy; a brother and sister reunite in Seattle to conduct an idiosyncratic memorial service for their father; a woman contemplates the family farm, located in the middle of contemporary San Francisco.

Valerie Miner has written ten previous books published by literary, academic and women's presses in the USA and the UK. Several of these stories have been broadcast on Radio 4, others published in *The Berkeley Fiction Review, Gargoyle* and other journals. "Miner is a writer of reach, audacity, range, uniquely important to understanding our time... She gives us the beat of everyday urban life" *Tillie Olsen* "Her exploration of the dynamics between friends is subtle, profoundly moving, and true." *Lisa Alther*. This is Valerie Miner's first book for Five Leaves.

Also Available in this Series

HOW DO YOU PRONOUNCE NULLIPAROUS?
by **Zoë Fairbairns**
160 pages, 0 907123 155, £7

Zoë Fairbairns' stories, set mainly in London and its more-or-less fashionable suburbs, occupy the spaces between words and actions, beliefs and realities. A 40-year-old woman who has never had children and never wanted to, revisits her decision; a little girl wonders why she attends a school run by a religion that neither she nor her parents belong to; 50-something lefties discover things that they might have preferred not to know about their pensions; a woman goes to meet her partner's new love, and tries to be friendly. The collection also includes an autobiographical piece reviewing the author's membership of a 1970s women's writing group.

Zoë Fairbairns' novels include *Benefits* (a feminist classic, re-published by Five Leaves), *Closing, Here Today, Stand We At Last, Other Names* and *Daddy's Girls*. Her short stories have appeared in many anthologies and have been broadcast on BBC Radio 4. She lives in London and works for a TV facilities company, subtitling programmes for deaf and hard-of-hearing viewers.

Also Available in this Series

FALSE RELATIONS by Michelene Wandor
160 pages, 0907123 201, £7

Michelene Wandor's new collection of short stories ranges from Biblical to modern, from Renaissance Italy to present day Israel, and from the power of music to its dangers. Her poetic and dramatic skills infuse her stories with vivid voices and haunting characters. Henry VIII and Isabella d'Este enjoy a clandestine encounter; a modern retelling of the Book of Esther liberates the voice of Queen Vashti; today's musicians encounter the old myths of Orpheus; and the dilemmas of being Jewish are poignantly traced through the European diaspora into the cross-cultural crises of the Middle East.

Michelene Wandor is a poet, playwright, musician and critic, as well as a prolific writer of short stories. Her dramatisation of Eugene Sue's *The Wandering Jew* was staged at the National Theatre. She won an International Emmy for her adaptation of *The Belle of Amherst* for Thames TV. She teaches creative writing at London Metropolitan University. Her selected poems, *Gardens of Eden Revisited*, are published by Five Leaves.